RESCUED BY HER
FIRE FIGHTER

GENEVIEVE TURNER

Chapter 1

"OH MY GOD, IT'S YOU." Beatriz Schuler clapped her hand across her mouth, but it was too late. She already looked like a complete idiot and she'd only just stepped out of her car.

The San Jacinto Mountain Wilderness Area in all its rough, wild glory spread out as far as she could see. The scent of pine and sage wrapped around her, and the ever-present sound of the wind gently brushed past her ears.

But she couldn't appreciate any of it thanks to the wickedly hot firefighter leaning against the truck parked at the trailhead.

Had he heard her? If not, maybe she could pretend she hadn't said anything, could pretend they hadn't had a crazy blind-date/one-night-stand several months ago.

Please. Please, God.

But to her utter horror, recognition was dawning across his face. "Bea?" His brows drew together. "Is that right?"

That had been part of the game of the date—no last names, no guarantee that they'd given their real names. No personal details. The only goal was to have fun. And she had, until she'd gotten drunk, sang horrible karaoke, and slept with him. Then never called him again.

This might be her worst nightmare come true, having him meet her at the trailhead.

His boots crunched in the red dirt as he came over to her, an expression of heart-stopping intensity on his face, his body all coiled, springing power.

"Um"—she held out her hand, trying to regain some sense of professionalism—"it's Beatriz. Beatriz Schuler."

He shook it, his hand large enough to engulf hers with space left over. "Oh. Luke called you Bea. And that's what you called yourself. Before." His voice matched his eyes, whiskey dark and mellow as the smoothest single malt. "I'm Russell Cheng. Russ."

She pulled her hand back. "Well, Luke's my cousin. He gets to use my nickname."

Crap. Now she was making it sound like *he* didn't get to use her nickname, which she'd kind of rather he didn't since she was already so anxious around him, but it was rude to point it out. She didn't do well in new social situations under any circumstances, but this was particularly agonizing.

"So you really are Russ?" That was the name he'd given her on the date. Apparently the two of them hadn't been as good at pretending to be someone else as they'd tried to be.

"Yep. And I'm here to lead you on this hiking trip." He said it as if he were honestly enthused about the idea.

Jeez, he had an amazing smile. Friendly, but with heat. Heat that made her toes want to curl in her hiking boots. Which was a huge problem since she was going to be alone with him for the next three days.

She rubbed her palms on her jeans. "Yes. That's right."

She put on her best professor voice. "I have a permit to collect some nightshade penstemon for my research. Luke recommended you as a suitable guide." Her tone was prissy enough to have even her wincing inwardly, but she needed him to stop smiling at her like that.

"I'll get you back safe and sound." He kept on smiling, damn it. "I got the coordinates you e-mailed me. It won't be an easy hike, but we should make it there in a day." He was amazingly self-assured, as if this was just any other meeting for him.

He was really too casual about all this. It made her anxiety even worse that he wasn't uneasy, but she needed that plant, and he'd been hired to guide her.

All right, she could be professional here. They'd had an unfortunate first meeting—okay, blind date—but they could move past it without ever mentioning it.

The wind kicked up, blasting her cheeks with chill and sending a large hank of hair into her mouth. She fished it out, trying not to grimace. So much for looking composed. "Great," she said. "Let me get my gear from the car and we can set off."

Bea poked her head into the front passenger side of her sedan and took several deep breaths. The air was thick with the scent of sage, which helped to clear her head. She'd been so looking forward to this trip—not only to get her plants, but because she loved these mountains. If the university where her lab was located weren't so far away, she'd be hiking here every weekend.

She grabbed the metal-framed backpack, her arm flexing hard against the weight of it, and hauled it out. As it hit the gravel of the trailhead parking lot, she heard him coming up behind her.

"Need help?" he asked.

"Nope." She spun to face him, tilting her head back in order to look up and up at him, then hefted the backpack onto her shoulders in one easy move. "See? I've got it."

Rather than being put off, his gaze went appreciative. "I can see."

"Shall we go?" Was that a *squeak* in her voice? Dear God. She started off for the trail, needing to get away from him. *Three days.* She could survive three days.

"Hang on."

She stopped, tried not to groan. The sooner they got on the trail, the sooner this could all be over. She put on a blandly inquiring expression as she turned back. "Yes?"

He had one hand in the pocket of his cargo shorts, the other running through his inky black hair. *Superfine Southern California dude at his leisure,* Bea would call that pose. "I've got to get my own pack," he said, "lock up the truck—Oh, and get Jax."

"Jax?" The twinkle in his eye made her suspect he was telling some kind of joke.

He opened his truck door and whistled. A beautiful Australian shepherd bounded out, with a close-clipped coat and a gorgeous set of eyes—one blue, one gold. He approached her calmly, intelligence shining from his clear gaze.

"Oh." She didn't care if she sounded dumbstruck—this was a glorious dog. "Can I pet him?"

"Sure."

At that, Jax began to wag his butt, coming toward her with his tongue lolling. She sank her hands into his fur, still thick despite his clip. And so soft—was there anything softer on earth?

"Aren't you amazing?" she asked the dog.

The glint in his mismatched eyes told her he understood and agreed.

"You like dogs?" Russ asked.

She knew what he meant: *You're more of a cat person.* Because she was prickly and cold. Of course a woman like her would like cats and shun dogs.

She might be prickly and cold, but she *was* a dog person. "I love them. But I can't have a dog in my condo. I have two cats instead."

Being a dog person didn't mean she couldn't appreciate cats too. But a dog like this... She could only dream. She ran a hand down the silk of his ears, and he cocked his head at her as if to ask, *Why so sad?*

Because I can't have a dog like you.

"Give me a minute to get loaded up, and we'll head off."

She watched as Russ pulled a backpack out of the bed of his truck, the muscles in his shoulders and back rippling beneath the dark gray cotton of his T-shirt. Her hand stilled on the dog's neck as her mouth went dry.

He crouched beside the pack, throwing his ass in sharp relief, and started going through the pockets. "You know, when Luke said his cousin needed a guide for a backpacking trip, he didn't say it was you."

He spoke the words as if they were old friends and not awkward acquaintances. He wanted her to like him. Bea had noticed that about him from the first. The pressure in his smile, the expectation in his jokes. He wanted to be liked.

Bea disliked that need of his. She never liked anyone on sight—she took her own good time to come around to someone and wouldn't be forced into it. And why did she need to like him or laugh at his jokes? They were here to fulfill a task. They didn't have to be friends.

Not that she was unfriendly—she only needed time, needed to know a person before she could unbend with them. But he'd proven on their date that he had the natural gift of setting people at ease.

And she'd ended up proving that enough alcohol overcame even *her* unease with new people. Enough to have her climbing into bed with him.

"Luke doesn't know about our... *date*." She ignored the burning in her cheeks. "At least, I didn't tell him."

She hadn't told anyone. She'd simply crawled out of Russ's bed the next day and raced home to nurse her aching head. On Monday she was back to being Professor Schuler —a woman who never bedded strange men, no matter how charming they were.

He gave her an unclouded look. "I don't kiss and tell." He said it as if it were a private joke between them.

She didn't like his refusal to be awkward. His attitude made her own sharpness that much keener, as if she had to be the black nastiness to his light sunniness.

But it hadn't been like that when they'd met before...

He'd shown up on her doorstep out of the blue all those months ago, startling her when she'd opened the door to find a very handsome, completely strange man on her doorstep.

"Lyla sent me," he'd said, as if that explained everything.

After some sputtering from the both of them, it had come out that Lyla had bid on him at a charity bachelor auction, Lyla being an old school acquaintance of Bea's. Once she'd won Russ for a night, Lyla suddenly realized that a married woman probably shouldn't be going out with a devastatingly hot firefighter, charity or no.

So she'd sent him over to Bea as a... prank? A gift? Bea

never was quite clear on that since she'd decided to stop speaking to Lyla at that very moment.

Bea apologized for his wasted time and had been that close to shutting the door on him when he'd convinced her to go out with him.

"Just something fun," he'd said. "No last names, no personal details. Just you and me having a good time."

Looking into the intoxicating warmth of his gaze, she'd almost been convinced. But— "No, really. I am sorry you came all this way and wasted all that time—"

"Do you like hot pot?"

That had done it, the slight dare in his words. A suggestion that no normal person would turn down hot pot, which involved cooking your own meal right at the table. Who wouldn't love that?

Bea might be reserved and a little stiff, but she wasn't abnormal. So she'd said yes.

Now here they were again, about to be trapped together for three days in the woods. God, if only she'd shut the door on him that night, things would have been so much easier. This was precisely why she had rules, *rules she didn't break.*

She wanted so badly to call the whole thing off, to get back into her car and never see him again. *Really* never see him again this time.

But she desperately needed her penstemon blooms. Otherwise she could kiss her career good-bye.

Well, she had only herself to blame. There was a good lesson here on why she shouldn't mix plum wine and sake and karaoke and one hot Chinese-American firefighter.

She gave Jax one last pat and straightened up. "If you didn't tell and I didn't tell, then no one knows. And we don't have to talk about it."

He worked his jaw. That had gotten through to him. "Okay." He slung his pack onto his back. "Let's go then."

He brushed past her without even a smile, which told her how irritated he was. Fine. Whatever. He didn't need to be talking about stuff that wouldn't happen again and had no bearing on their present situation. Stuff that made her unbearably uneasy.

Jax fell in behind Russ, leaving her to bring up the rear. Which gave her a pretty good view of Russ's rear.

His shirt was tight, molded to muscles that he must spend quite a bit of time honing in the gym. He looked completely capable of carrying a full-grown person to safety on those broad shoulders. Of course he would be exactly the body type she was attracted to—not too bulky, but clearly a strong man.

Jax stopped and threw her a look as if he knew what she was thinking. He might—he was a smart dog. Or maybe all the ladies who were treated to this view had the same thoughts she did.

"You're here to collect a plant?" Russ's question had her snapping her gaze to anywhere but his ass. "Are you a botanist?"

"Um..." She finally settled on her feet as the safest place for her to look. "No, I'm a neuroscientist. I need a chemical that's present in the blooms of the plant."

"Hmm. Nightshade penstemon. I don't think I've ever heard of it."

"It's fairly rare. It only grows at a certain elevation and only in these mountains. It's small, very low to the ground, with tiny pink blooms." She looked out over the chamisal surrounding them. It would be impossible to see any of her penstemon from here, not that they were even at the right spot. The chamise was too tall, its sprays of white blooms and spiny leaves hiding everything beneath. "A ranger found a fairly large field of them last year and marked down the coordinates because it's endangered."

"That's where we're going? They might not be there this year."

"I know. But it's the only chance I have."

"Why do you need this particular plant so badly?"

She could hear the faint note of censure there—*why are you killing an endangered species?*

"Science. It very specifically binds and activates the mu1-opioid receptor."

"Huh."

She recognized the unfocused quality to that noise, which signaled deep disinterest, but she was already winding up. "Yes, this subunit—" *Stop it, Bea. Stop it.* She took a deep breath, pulling herself out of lecture mode. "We've tried everything to get it to grow in the lab, but we haven't been successful, and we can't synthesize the compound. I do have a permit, and I'm only taking five pounds. If there were any way to get it other than harvesting the plant, I wouldn't be here."

He said nothing. Clearly she hadn't convinced him of the importance of this. Discovering an entirely new class of opioids—which was possible with the compound from the plant—could revolutionize pain management in medicine. Maybe she could try that. Or maybe she should just stop lecturing.

"Therefore, I need to harvest the blooms," she finished. No sense telling him how many careers were riding on this plant—including her own. This compound could make her career and that of everyone in her lab. But nonscientists never understood such things. Or Bea wasn't good at explaining them. Science was a language all its own, and she'd never been a very good translator.

Either way, he only needed to know that she had to have this plant. And she was legally allowed to take five pounds of it.

"Usually the people I bring up are here to enjoy themselves."

The dab of criticism there had her back stiffening. "I'm not here to have fun." *Or be friends. Or sleep with you again.*

Jax stopped to nudge at her hand with his wet nose. She ran her hand over his head, along the silk of his ears.

I'll take your dog. But you, Mr. Sexy Firefighter, can keep your nudges to yourself.

RUSS KNEW it was going to be a long, cold trip.

Take my cousin up to the wilderness area, Luke had said to Russ. *She's an experienced hiker—it'll be easy.*

He owed Luke for the bar incident the weekend before anyway, so he'd agreed easily enough. Luke was a fun guy, always up for a good time. Why wouldn't his cousin be the same?

Boy, was Russ wrong! It could have been the one-night-stand thing hanging between them, but she was not happy. She didn't want to be friends or even friendly. She just wanted her five pounds of endangered plant. From the way she'd said it, he guessed she had a scale in her backpack and was going to weigh out exactly 5.0000 pounds of the stuff.

He'd taken some serious, reserved people out before, but no one as reserved as Bea. She'd wanted to give him a lecture on her work. He could hear the rest of what she wanted to say lurking in the spaces between what she *had* said.

He had a talent for reading people. And people liked him, which he intended them to. He'd learned that early in his childhood, going from America to Taiwan and back again, having to adjust his entire world every time. Putting people at ease, ensuring that they enjoyed being around him, making sure they liked him made him feel easier and happier himself. It let him adjust immediately to any situation, which was a needed skill both during childhood and in his job.

Having *her* dislike him made him itch deep beneath his skin. Their steamy night was going to be a minefield here.

Jax liked her though. And she really liked Jax. So there was that. Maybe if Russ gave her a little time, a little space, she'd realize things didn't need to be weird between them. That she could be easy with him without worrying he might bring up what had happened before. Then the situation would be comfortable for the both of them.

She'd been stiff at the beginning of their date too—only it was an embarrassed kind of stiff. He'd felt bad that her friend had done that to her, and he'd wanted to make her feel better. Once she'd loosened up, she'd been funny in a sharp, sarcastic kind of way—his favorite kind of way. *He* wanted things to be easy and happy, for people to be comfortable with him—but she clearly wasn't afraid to put some burn on her words. He admired that.

They'd had a great time. She'd laughed through hot pot, sang some terrible karaoke that she'd been drunk enough to think was awesome, and then... they'd ended up in bed together.

His skin heated at the memory. She had the slender build of a ballet dancer, but her movements had a controlled fierceness like she had volcanoes going off in her mind and was holding the eruptions in. She hadn't held anything back that night though.

Luke had said she was smart. Russ had guessed that from their date, although he couldn't ask her about it—he'd agreed to no personal information to help put her at ease. But judging by her little lecture, she was more than smart.

He glanced back at her. "Doing okay?"

Her face was flushed, a deepening rose staining her cheeks and making her skin dewy. But she was totally comfortable with it. Maybe she was getting more relaxed with him. "I'm fine," she said. "I've missed hiking."

"You can come up any weekend, you know."

Her expression flattened. Jesus, he'd only meant that she ought to get out more, not proposition her.

"I have to work."

As if he didn't have to, too. Also, this *was* work for him, taking people up here. A side job from his firefighting gig, but he got paid. "Become a hiking guide," he said. "You get to hike on weekends and call it work."

And hang out with new people, learn more about all kinds of walks of life—it was a perfect sideline for him.

There might have been a glint of amusement in her eyes, but she ducked her head before he could fully savor it. "Shouldn't we be to the trail fork by now?"

Listen to her, as if she were the guide here. "We'll hit it in another thirty minutes."

"But the schedule—"

God, she was one of those. She'd probably charted the route on Google Maps and calculated how long it would take to get to the fork using "an average person's speed." Her kind was always the hardest to guide since they got real antsy when things didn't happen when they thought they should.

"Sometimes things don't happen on schedule." He kept his tone free of his annoyance.

Which only got her back up. To be fair, he'd put some extra lazy drawl into his voice. She was probably writing him off as sloppy and careless even now.

"Well, if we want to find these plants before the weekend's over, we'll need to pick up the pace."

A sudden realization hit him. "Are you tracking our progress on the GPS on your phone?"

"Yes. Am I not allowed to do that?"

"You can do whatever you like." Keeping the client happy was the second rule of being a guide. First was to keep them safe.

"Aren't you doing the same?"

"I have my phone and it has GPS, but no, I'm not." He couldn't stand the thought of having his phone glued to his hand as he hiked. "I know the trail, know where we need to end up—and I'm just enjoying the rest."

"I told you—"

"You're not here to have fun. I know." So much for getting her to relax. He jerked his chin at her. "Jax wants some petting."

Without hesitating, she rubbed the dog's ears.

He swung his head to hide his smile. Definitely a sucker for dogs. Beautiful, sexy, smart, and a sucker for dogs. He had to get her to unwind again. And maybe, maybe, if they got comfortable enough with each other, he could ask her why she'd never called.

"Why don't you tell me more about your work?" That ought to please her.

She started off again, and he only understood about half

of it. It wasn't that he was dumb—although plenty of people assumed that about firefighters—but more that she was speaking an entirely different language. If he slipped into Mandarin, no doubt she'd feel like he did just now.

Or maybe not Mandarin. She seemed like the kind of woman who'd picked up some Mandarin here and there. Taiwanese then.

He glanced back at her every so often to check that she was doing all right. But she seemed to be doing better than fine. She was still going on about her work, but she moved with an easy strength. She might be one of the most physically fit women he'd ever guided, which he hadn't been expecting when he'd heard what she did. Weren't scientists pasty and lanky?

Of course, scientists probably had as many myths about them going around as firefighters did.

They reached the fork ahead of schedule, both of them breathing a touch harder. But it felt good to be out in the wide open with his heart pumping and the wind whipping around him.

He sent her an easy grin, feeling triumphant. "See? Made it with time to spare."

She didn't grin back. "Well, that's good."

"Still checking your phone?"

Her mouth twitched. "No. It's too beautiful out here to be looking at a screen."

He didn't bother to say *I told you so*. He didn't want to piss her off any further. "All right. Now we start to climb. You ready?"

She adjusted her backpack and craned her head as she looked up at the peak. "Yep."

He let her go ahead since she was so eager. And so he could get a quick view of her rear. Ungentlemanly of him, but goddamn, did she have a nice ass. A girl as slender as she was shouldn't have such a shapely ass. Maybe she did that booty yoga.

Jax gave a short bark as if to say *Done?*

"Huh," he said softly to the dog. "As if you aren't half in love with her yourself."

Not that Russ really was. But man, did she intrigue him. Especially with the way she blew hot and cold. She was all coldness here, but on their date—

"Are you coming?"

Definitely cold here. "Yeah," he called back. "Had to adjust my pack."

They followed the trail leading northwest, climbing toward the elevation where her precious penstemon grew. She was able to keep up a fair clip—at this pace they might even be back half a day early. A damn shame since that was half a day he wouldn't get to try to crack her shell again. He wanted to hear her laugh, just once.

She'd done plenty of laughing on their date. And telling jokes and enjoying herself—he wanted to see that Bea again. He wanted to spend time with that woman, if only for a few days, to have her enjoy spending time with him too.

As they hiked on, she didn't check her phone once, and he was pleased to see her finally unwinding even that little bit.

But three hours later they came to a dead stop.

What looked like about half a hillside was strewn across the trail, boulders and tree roots poking haphazardly up from the pile, which was entirely blocking their way forward.

"A landslide." She sounded as if nature had slapped her full across the face. "How could there be a landslide?"

"We had a hard rain a week ago. This sometimes

happens. With the budget cuts, not everything in the wilderness area gets fixed right away." He wondered if a park ranger had even checked this trail yet. It wasn't a popular route, so probably not. *Shit.*

"How do we get around?" She put a hand to her eyes as she looked toward the summit, no doubt thinking of simply going straight up the mountain face.

"Not by going that way." She was a good hiker, but not that good. Neither was he. "We'll have to backtrack to the fork and take the other trail. It's harder going and will take longer, but we'll get there in the end."

He really didn't want to take the alternate path—not only was it harder going, it was used even less than this trail. They might come across yet another landslide there. But if he was going to get her to those plants, they'd have to.

"How much longer will it take?" She was completely undaunted. Well, he'd guessed she had a one-track mind.

"A day. At least."

She was not happy about that, her mouth pinching into a thin line. Maybe she wanted to turn around.

He ought to encourage her to do that. When he said the trail was rough, he wasn't exaggerating—she'd have a tough time of it no matter how much time she spent in the gym. Booty yoga could only take her so far out here.

Keep her safe—taking that trail would skirt dangerously close to breaking the first rule. "We can turn around too," he offered. "Try again another time."

Judging by the slight recoil of her head, she wasn't happy about that idea either. Hell, he got it—she was uncomfortable about their past. But geez, he hadn't brought it up again, just like she'd wanted. She could cut him a break here.

"Whatever you want to do, we'll do it." He gave her his winningest smile.

"I want to get this plant. And I want it now." She turned and started marching. "Let's go the longer route then."

He smiled at her retreating back. He'd give her points for fortitude at least.

And now he had one whole day more with her. Best to make the most of it.

Chapter 2

FOR ALL THAT THEY WERE out in the middle of nowhere, Bea found that gaining some privacy was damned difficult.

They'd made camp—where she wasn't quite sure since they were so far off the route they should be on—but they'd found a nice clearing and set up the tents and eaten the meal Russ warmed up on the camping stove. A campfire couldn't be risked even with the recent rain. And fires set outside designated areas in the wilderness area were a no-go anyway. So no s'mores for them.

Bea could do without the s'mores. She wanted to find a private place to make a call, somewhere Russ couldn't hear her. But of course with no door to shut and no room to hide in, her voice would carry pretty far. And she couldn't slip into the tent and be muttering into the phone. That would look weird, and she didn't want that.

Therefore a hike into the brush was required. She said something about needing a moment—he could make of that what he wished—and pushed her way into the chamisal.

They'd spent most of the day among the junipers and

piñon, but they'd dropped in elevation near the end of the day; the low, tough scrub surrounding them was proof of that. Spiky, sparse, and a dull greenish-brown, these plants were meant to survive desert conditions. The rain they'd gotten wasn't recent enough to turn the scrub green. But give it a few days…

Any more disasters like today and they might be here to see everything go green. She let herself groan aloud since there was no one to hear. Multiple days of being tormented by the nearness of Russ… She shivered beneath her jacket and tugged her hat over her ears. It got so cold up here at night, even at the lower elevations.

The chamisal thinned and a likely space opened up before her. Perfect. She pulled out her phone, checked the signal. Three bars. *Not bad. Don't let me lose the signal entirely.*

First she checked her e-mail. Work always had to come first, her personal emotional crises second. There were a few things that would keep until she got back. Next was an e-mail from Kelly, one of the grad students, about an experiment that wasn't working. Bea fired off a few suggestions and told her they'd meet when she returned. And then the final one from her lab manager: *the ultracentrifuge needs repairs.*

She let her groan be loud and long. That was going to be expensive, and that stupid 'fuge was always breaking. Yet more money from her grants gone toward it. She authorized the repairs in her message back and tried not to dwell on the cost. She might pass out if she did.

Afterward she called up Lil's number, waited through a ring. And another. And another. *Come on, Lil. I need you.*

"Hello? Bea?"

Thank you, God. "Lil. Lil, I'm here." Hearing her cousin's voice was... it was an anchor in all this mess. Bea wanted to cling to it.

"What's wrong?"

What wasn't wrong? Bea rubbed at her nose. *Don't start crying.* "I'm fine." She cleared her throat. "How are you? How's the bed rest?"

"Boooring."

Bea smiled. Of course Lil would be climbing the walls. "And, uh, Adriano?"

A beat. "He's... It's... Yeah, it's a little weird." Lil's voice dropped as if she didn't want him to overhear. "We're living together, but it's completely platonic and..."

"And it's driving you mad." This would be a perfect place for Bea to point out that Lil and Adriano were perfect for each other—oh, and there was also the small matter of the baby they were having together—but Lil was more stubborn than a mule. She'd have to figure it out herself before she believed it.

"I guess. I don't know," Lil said. Bea could feel her shrug across the line. "How about you? How are things going with Fireman Goofy?"

Not this. "Don't call him that." It had been Lil's idea of a joke to refer to her unknown guide as "Fireman Goofy" before the trip. It was especially not funny now that Bea knew who Russ really was.

Lil chuckled evilly. "Fooled you, didn't I? He's so hot. And you're alone with him."

"It's not like that." She couldn't help the snap in her words.

"Whoa. I was just kidding. Bea, what's wrong?"

Bea hunched her shoulders and pinched the bridge of her nose, which burned with unshed tears. "There was a landslide. Not recently—we're fine. But we had to take a longer route. We'll be here another day."

"Oh. Well, an extra day out shouldn't be so bad." Lil was right; it shouldn't be. But it was so, so bad. "Unless Russ is getting on your nerves?"

He was, but not in the way Lil thought. More in an "I want you to make my nerves explode with pleasure again" kind of way.

Time to confess all, which was the real reason Bea had called. "Remember that blind date I went on a while back?"

"You did?" Lil snapped her fingers. "Oh, I remember. You didn't like him or something or you didn't hit it off. I wasn't surprised—I'm not sure why you went on a blind date at all." A sharp gasp. "Wait, that was Russ?"

Bea didn't need to worry about keeping her face warm— her cheeks were flaming. "Yeah."

"Oh, Bea, so you went out with him on one mediocre date. It's not a big deal, so don't make it one." Of course Lil would say that—she blew through men like a Santa Ana wind. "And why didn't you tell me this when you went out with him? Or when you knew he was taking you on this trip?"

"I didn't know who he was." If Bea had, she certainly wouldn't have had him lead her into the wilderness. And Lil might change her tune after this next bit: "I didn't tell you everything about that date."

A long beat of silence where Lil was probably filling in who knew what details. "Oh. Well, you'd probably better now."

How to start the sordid tale? Bea wrapped her free arm around herself, searching for warmth. "Lyla won him in a charity auction."

God, that sounded bad. As if Russ were an escort.

"What does that have to do with it?"

Bea closed her eyes. "Just... just let me finish. It gets *convoluted* at times. She won a night out with him, but she didn't want to go on the date. So she sent him to my door."

"Oh, Bea." Sympathy dripped from Lil's words—she knew exactly how Bea would have greeted that. "That was really crappy of Lyla. But how did you end up going out with him? And not slamming the door in his face?"

How many times had Bea asked herself that question? "He convinced me." As simple and as complicated as that.

It had been a Friday night, she had nowhere to be—why not open that bottle of Malbec she'd been saving? Then she'd opened her door to find a smoking-hot fireman claiming to be her bought-and-paid-for date for the evening. No wonder she'd gone a little crazy.

He'd taken her to hot pot, which was always fun, no matter who you were with.

Or maybe the sake she'd steadily imbibed made it fun. One cup had made her feel witty and relaxed. So why not two and become even more relaxed? And so on, until everything was a happy haze. There had even been karaoke at one point.

After, when he'd been taking her home, she'd blurted out, "Can we go to your place?" Because his smile had warmed her from the inside out, and she'd had a great time with him, and she was very, very, *very* attracted to him.

She distinctly remembered falling into his bed, reaching up for him as his weight came over her. It had been good— she hadn't been too drunk to have great sex.

And then came the morning after.

With her head throbbing fit to burst and stomach rolling like she was on the high seas, she'd awoken underneath him, his arm tucking her into his side and a heavy thigh pinning her legs down. God, but he'd been solid.

Embarrassment like she'd never known flamed across her skin next. She couldn't remember everything she'd done the night before, but she did remember that he'd been so *nice*. Maybe she'd been a horrible, sloppy drunk, and he'd only been humoring her.

And he'd been paid to do it. Or auctioned off. Or something. And she'd asked him to take her to his place.

The date had been fun, the sex had been explosive—and she'd never know if that was because Russ actually liked her as a person, or if he was just going along with their game. For Bea, who knew she wasn't a "fun, likable" person, that knowledge had been utterly intolerable.

She'd slipped out without waking him, thank the Lord, and erased his number from her phone.

But that hadn't stopped her from turning the memory of that night over and over in her mind, the shame of it all still sharp enough to slice even all these months later.

Lil's noise of admiration pulled Bea back to the present. "He must be good if he convinced you."

You have no idea. "He suggested that we not share any personal info. That we just enjoy ourselves."

"You didn't talk about work?"

"No. And I can talk about other things." That stung coming from Lil, who'd had many conversations with Bea about everything but work. "I didn't know his full name, he didn't know mine. All I knew was that his name was Russ and he was a hot firefighter who liked to sell himself for charity."

"What charity?" Lil asked.

"Oh. Foster kids. Buying them winter coats, school supplies, things like that."

"That's..." Lil's voice went suspiciously wobbly. "That's really sweet."

Her normally unflappable cousin was being turned inside out by pregnancy. To be honest, Bea was touched too. If she had to have a terrible blind date, at least some kids in need got something out of it. "Yes, well, he's not a bad guy. Not at all." It might have been easier if he was, since he'd deserve her prickliness then.

"So what's the problem?"

Jesus, could Lil really not put two and two together? Was Bea going to have to spell the whole thing out? "I drank too much. I sang karaoke. And I slept with him."

Utter, shocked silence. And then: "Wow. Okay, I see now."

The tears threatened again. "Yeah." Bea released a shaky breath and hugged herself tighter.

"Did he... does he remember?"

"Yeah."

"Did he say anything?"

"Not really. I might have told him I didn't want to talk about it." And he'd held to that, thank God. Although the awkwardness remained, at least on Bea's end.

"Huh. So he was that bad in bed?"

"*No.* He's... Look, I'm sure he's Mr. July in the fireman's calendar—the hottest month of the year."

Lil didn't laugh, not that Bea had really been expecting her to. "That's what's got you upset. Not that he did anything wrong, but that you embarrassed yourself with him... and you still really like him."

That... that wasn't it at all. "I'm only here to get my plant, not have awkward run-ins with a one-night stand. That is the point—the definition—of a one-night stand. One night!"

"Yeah, God forbid anyone see you as a flawed human."

"Lil!" First the comment about not being able to talk about anything but work and then this... Bea was almost regretting this call.

"Sorry." Lil's voice went wobbly again. "I didn't mean that—I know how tough that kind of stuff is for you. It's just... I'm stuck on the couch, things with Adriano are so flipping weird, Luke is up to something and he won't say what... I wish you were here instead of stuck in the wilderness with your embarrassing past."

"Me too." And suddenly Bea was happy that she'd called her cousin. It was nice to be wanted.

"When do you think you'll be back?" The need in Lil's voice tugged at Bea's heart. She really did wish she could be there for her cousin.

"It should be Tuesday now instead of Monday." Bea sent up a silent prayer that it wouldn't take any longer.

"Need me to take care of the cats?"

"You're on bed rest, remember? And I already texted Mia." Bea knew she'd sound silly with this, but she had to get it out: "He has a really awesome dog."

"Better than Rufio?"

Because she knew it would tweak Lil, Bea said, "Yep. Super-smart. And the softest fur ever." It was true. If only Russ had been a lout without an awesome dog... But then she probably wouldn't have gone on a blind date with him in the first place.

"Rufio's smart." Lil couldn't say anything about his fur since he was a terrier. "Bea, it sounds like you really like this guy. And his dog. Maybe you should reconsider."

A shiver ran across Bea's skin and not at all because of the cold. "A hiking trip is no place to find out if a guy is a good match."

"Really?"

Bea didn't point out that Lil was an example of how even having a baby with a man wasn't a good way to test making it for the long haul. "No. Because once we get back and he sees how much I work and that I mostly eat takeout and that I need things a certain way... Yeah."

It wasn't that things *had* to be exactly how she liked them; it just made her life so much more pleasant when they were. She'd learned the hard way that most men wanted things to be exactly how *they* liked them. Which was why she'd didn't make the effort to date—it wasn't worth the trouble.

"But you both like hiking," Lil said. "So there's that."

"That's not enough." Bea meant to be jovial, but it only came out sad. "Look, I'm freezing out here in the open. I'll call you tomorrow. You get some rest."

"God, you sound like Adriano."

Lil might be exasperated, but Bea was glad someone was taking care of her cousin. "Don't get too mad," she warned. "You've got to watch your blood pressure."

Lil made a rude noise but signed off with, "I love you, coz."

"Love you."

Bea disconnected the call and stared at the phone for a moment, a slight smile curving her mouth. She did feel better—but Lil was wrong about liking Russ. Or reconsidering her stance on dating him again. Not that he even wanted to.

She turned on the phone's flashlight app and marched off for more of the torment of his company.

RUSS'S HEART lightened when Jax barked. Bea must be coming back to camp.

He knew she needed some space, especially after the shock of seeing him again, but he'd worried when she'd been out there. There were bears and mountain lions in these mountains. Once she was out of sight, he immediately regretted not sending Jax with her. *Keep her safe.* The first rule, and he couldn't do it if he didn't know where she was. But she was back.

She was huddled in her jacket, gloves covering her hands and a sleek knit cap covering her dark, chin-length hair. He could still remember the ticklish sensation of her hair trailing along his jaw as they'd kissed. He'd like to kiss her now, to pull her down next to him and cuddle close to her, sharing warmth and kisses under the stars.

He knew that idea would not be well received though.

They had no camp chairs, so she sat on the bare ground outside her tent, half facing Russ. Jax came over to nuzzle against her, and she rubbed the dog's ears.

Russ would have called the dog a traitor, but since he wanted to do the same himself, it'd be a bit hypocritical.

"Find what you needed?" he asked.

"Yeah." Short but not curt.

He wondered if she'd called Luke to chew him out for the situation he'd put them in. Not that it was Luke's fault—the guy didn't know. And she didn't strike Russ as the chewing-out type. She'd be coldly furious and give a person the silent treatment, not yell and shout. And once she'd thawed, she'd discuss the whole thing rationally.

It'd be interesting to find out. He was only getting the cold shoulder, so maybe it was wishful thinking on his part that she'd thaw.

But he had something to warm her up. "Want some hot chocolate? It's the really fancy kind."

"Fancy, huh? How could I refuse?" Her half smile was the most genuine expression he'd seen on her so far this trip.

He passed the mug over and she wrapped her hands around it, taking a deep sniff, the tip of her thin nose pink with cold.

Good. That would warm her and maybe even loosen her up too. He wanted her to let go of some of the tension holding her so tightly. Yeah, this was a work trip for her, and their first encounter was hanging between them... but she should relax.

She took a sip and then closed her eyes. "Mmm."

Close enough to a groan to have him shifting uncomfortably. He focused on his own mug. "It gets cold up here. Sometimes hot chocolate is the only way to get warm."

"That was a good idea."

"Thanks. I occasionally have them."

She went red. "Sorry. I know that I can be difficult, but you're the expert here. I don't mean to seem like I'm questioning you."

"I was only making a joke." She was so sensitive, as if she were carrying around an exposed nerve. "I don't think you're difficult." He was gratified to see that surprised her. "And I don't think you can help it."

"Help what?"

"Questioning things."

She peered into her mug, swirling the contents around. "Well, it does help in my line of work."

"But you think it annoys people." He wasn't certain if he should put that as a question or a statement, but given how skittish she'd been when he'd appeared on her doorstep, he guessed she was a naturally reserved person.

"It does," she insisted. "You're right, I can't help it—but it can come off as arrogant. Imagine if you were trying to put out a fire and I kept questioning what you were doing."

"But I'm not putting out a fire here. We're only hiking." They were actually doing quite a bit more, talking like this in the deepening dark. He felt her slipping away from her earlier antagonism... but not quite reaching the friendliness she'd had on the date.

"Do you do this every weekend?" she asked.

"Most weekends."

"You must like it then."

He could see there where some people might interpret that as challenging, as if she didn't believe that they could possibly like it. But he got the impression that wasn't what she meant—she wanted him to examine if he really did enjoy it and why. To prove to himself that he enjoyed it.

"Yep," was all he said, even though that wouldn't be much of an argument for her.

"How did you get started? I would think firefighting would be more than enough."

Firefighting was a demanding profession, especially keeping up with the paramedic certifications, but leading groups out here wasn't really work for him. "I used to come out here every weekend and just camp. No groups, no one else—only me and the mountains."

His parents had thought it odd—why did he need so much time alone? But after the high-tension environment of the fire station, there was something to be said for doing a thing simply because he liked it. And being alone while he did it.

"I feel like you're going to say something very profound

now," she said. Ah, there was that dry humor of hers. He'd missed it.

He laughed, because he had sounded pretty pretentious. "Nope, not me. Anyway, a buddy of mine wanted to take his wedding party out here instead of the usual bachelor-party stuff. He offered to pay me to lead them, help with supplies, make sure nobody died." He shrugged. "It just went on from there. It's more sharing my enjoyment of the mountains than the money. Most people come out looking to have a good time, and I like helping them make memories they'll enjoy."

That was about as philosophical as he got. He'd leave the probing questions to her.

"Most people?"

It figured she'd narrow in on that. "A few people get out here and find that camping isn't really for them. And there was one couple who decided that a hiking trip would help save their marriage." That had been a nightmare.

"And it didn't?"

"Nope. They were ready to sign the divorce papers by the time we'd hiked out." And they'd argued viciously the entire time. It had been his most miserable trip yet, and nothing he'd tried—and he'd tried everything—had made them stop slashing at each other. "The wilderness... it whittles people and things to their essentials. If the essential part of a person isn't meant to be with another, coming here will only reveal the depth of the mismatch, not heal it."

"That's very philosophical." She gestured with the mug, her movements more expansive, her voice brighter. "Perhaps you should offer marriage counseling."

Okay, maybe he *could* get more philosophical. "That one trip gave me my fill."

"If they'd stayed together, would that have changed your mind?"

He thought about it, taking a swig of his drink as he did. "You mean, what upsets me more? That they were fighting on their trip or that the trip didn't fix their relationship?"

"Yes."

She was quite possibly the most thoughtful person he'd ever spoken with. He could see how some people might be uncomfortable, but here, just the two of them under the stars, it seemed like this was the only kind of conversation to have. Anything else would be too shallow. "Well, how do you feel when your experiments fail?"

"The only way we learn is through failure. You discover the most critical steps of an experiment when it goes wrong."

"Huh. We've got a similar philosophy in firefighting." Not that they ever wanted anything to go wrong on a fire, but if it could help save others in the future, they studied it.

"How long have you been a firefighter?"

She was picking leaves and burrs from Jax's fur, the dog staring at her adoringly. Russ understood the impulse. He'd like to get those fingers of hers on his body too.

"About ten years," he said. "How long have you been a scientist?"

"Hmm." He didn't think it a hard question, but she thought on it a while. "Well," she said finally, "I got my first lab job as an undergrad about fifteen years ago. So I guess that's when I started doing science. But I was already a science major before that. Then on to grad school, then my postdoc, and I've been a professor for two years now. And the dreaded tenure decision is coming in a few years."

He didn't know much about science careers, but that

sounded intense. "So what exactly does this plant do? Go slower this time—I didn't quite get it the last time."

She stared into her mug. "I'm not very good at explaining these things."

The hesitance in her voice pricked at him—he should have listened more closely when she'd talked about it before. "But you're the only one on this trip who understands them."

"Okay." She nodded with resolve. "Okay, I can try again. Tell me if I'm losing you."

"I will."

She held up the cup between them. "Imagine that this is a receptor on a neuron. And when specific chemicals bind to it"—she made a ball of her fist and lowered it into the cup—"like this, then the neuron is activated. Or shut off. Opioids do that with pain neurons, turn them off."

"Okay. That makes sense." He already knew some of this from his paramedic training, but let her go on. Her animation and focus was endearing.

And she was relaxed.

"But using opioids for pain relief has side effects." She gave him a questioning look.

"Yeah, I know." He'd seen his fair share of addicts and overdoses in his work.

"Well, we know from our early experiments that the penstemon compound fits the receptor differently than other opioids." She mimed her hand dipping into the cup again. "So it might have different side effects. Less devastating side effects, which could help a lot of people."

Huh. This was actually pretty fascinating even if she weren't so into it, her eyes bright and the curve of her lips animated.

"Is that why you need this plant so badly?" he asked.

"Yes. Well, that and there are seven people in my lab, all depending on me for grants and to help write papers and to guide their research and their careers..." A gentle sigh. "Sometimes it's a lot."

She said it softly, but he could hear the weight in it. The pressure of expectations and responsibility that sat upon her.

He understood why she was deadly serious about her work. But she'd been funny on their date. In a tipsy kind of way, but really funny. And later, when she'd put her arms around his neck and asked him to take her to his place... He hadn't been laughing then.

"Why didn't you ever call?" He'd meant to take it slow, to work up to asking that, but remembering their night together—the memories forced the question out of him.

That surprised her, her eyes going wide enough for him to see the whites even in the moonlight. "What do you mean?"

She knew exactly what he meant, and it irritated him that she chose to play dumb.

"After our date. Why didn't you ever call me?"

"Because... because it wasn't a date." Her voice crackled with anxiety. "You were paid. And it was a prank on me."

And because she'd been embarrassed. He could tell by the harsh vibrations in her voice.

"It felt like a date." He kept his own tone neutral, neither pushing her forward nor pulling himself away.

"Pfft. I got sloppy drunk."

Ah, and she was angry at herself as well for losing control. "No, not too sloppy. You were sober enough to do karaoke. You sang some song about calling me darling. Or not calling me darling."

"I wasn't singing *darling* to you." Her words went clipped, her shoulders tensing.

He recalled her crooning into the mic, gesturing to him as she sang her heart out. As if she were singing only to him, a private performance with an audience of one. "It felt like it."

That deflated her. She stared into her mug for several moments, more sad than pensive. "If that's so, why didn't *you* call?"

A question he'd often asked himself. Because if he couldn't get her out of his mind—and she wasn't going to give him a call—what would it have hurt for him to make the move?

"Because you strike me as the kind of woman who does the pursuing," he said. "You don't want to be pursued." She reminded him of a cat like that. As soon as you said you love cats, the suckers hid under the bed. Claim that you hate cats, and they wouldn't leave your lap.

So he'd kept quiet, hoping she would read his noncommunication as "I hate cats" and clamber into his lap. But his gamble hadn't paid off.

Her reserve came crashing back, hard enough for him to feel it as body blow. So much for the progress he'd been making on relaxing her.

"I apologize again." As stiff as her shoulders. "I'm deeply embarrassed by the whole thing."

And I don't want you to talk about it anymore. He heard that part loud and clear from her body language. "You shouldn't be." She acted as if she'd stripped on the tables for the entire restaurant.

"The karaoke, what happened after... I never do that." Anger vibrated through her, but he knew it was directed at herself, not him. And that hurt more than if it had been sent his way.

"Never do karaoke? You should. You have a very"—he couldn't say good, because her voice wasn't—"a very passionate voice. And hardly anyone does country songs."

Her shoulders dropped. "Yeah, I was amazed David Allen Coe was even on the song list."

He suppressed his smile at the shift in her mood. "So you do remember?"

"Of course. I remember all of it." But clearly she didn't want to. "I was hoping you wouldn't."

"I wasn't drinking as much as you. That plum wine can be a killer. And the sake."

She covered her face with her hand. "I apologize. For all of it. Again."

He wanted to cross over to her, to pull her hand from her face and kiss it all better. To make her happy again. Instead, he said, "All of it? I hope not." He let his voice drop. "Because some of it was flipping amazing."

Come on. Remember some of the good stuff. The parts where we were naked together? Those were amazing.

"But I was drunk—"

"Still. You were amazing." The hesitation in her voice had him pouncing. *A little closer... you know you want to remember the rest.*

"Is that why you hoped I'd call?"

"Partly. Mostly so I could hear you do more country karaoke."

But she didn't laugh. Nor did she relax further. "That will never happen." She handed the mug back to him. "Thank you for the hot chocolate. You were right—it did warm me up."

But not enough. "Want some more?"

"If you're hoping I'll drink enough to sing, I'll have to disappoint you."

He smiled as he took the mug. An actual joke—they'd made some progress despite her backtracking. "Good night then. I'll see you in the morning."

She waved and disappeared into her tent.

He watched the stars as Jax came to sit next to him and Bea rustled about. He tried to identify all the constellations he knew and not think about what she might be doing or what clothes she might be taking off.

He wasn't very successful.

Chapter 3

BEA WANTED TO TURN BACK.

She wouldn't, but this was much, much harder than the first trail. Up, then down, and up again, and even a few boulders to climb—which Russ had helped her with—until she was panting, her legs burning. Even Jax was slowing down.

So she pushed harder. The sooner she could get her plants, the sooner she could get home.

They hadn't spoken much that morning, which she'd been grateful for. His admission last night that he'd wanted her to call... She didn't know what to do with that. It was like he'd handed her a bomb and told her to carry it the entire trip. It hadn't gone off yet, but it might. At any time.

She studied Russ's calves, his awesome calves, as they flexed with his movements. She might set that bomb off herself, so attractive did she find him. *Still* found him.

Tilting her head, she took another look at a different angle. He clearly worked out. And not any kind of vanity lifting—those were the calves of a man who'd hiked thousands of miles. Maybe he even did ultramarathons. The only other time she'd seen calves like those had been on an ultramarathoner. The muscles flexed again and her insides fluttered. Or shuddered—that was too hard to be a flutter.

Okay, maybe she should have called him after their date. Or at least not run off the morning after. But it felt like it was too late now. They'd passed that point, and they couldn't go back. And like she'd told Lil, a hiking trip was no place to learn if they were meant for a relationship.

He couldn't hear her, but arguing like this in her head with him was making her see that she was right. And if she could say these things to him, he'd agree.

The sooner Bea could get away from Russ and never see him again, the better. Because the sight of his legs was doing odd things to her equilibrium. She hadn't focused so much on his legs that night, but she definitely remembered how his ass had felt, clenching under her hands as he'd thrust into her. His cargo shorts were too loose to get another good view of his ass, which was a shame.

"Doing okay?" he asked.

"Fine." Breathless, but she got it out.

He nodded and kept on going. He checked in with her every fifteen minutes, asking how she was. He probably didn't realize that it was so regular, but she'd noticed.

Then he varied his question. "Having fun?" he called back.

Ah, the silent portion of the morning was over and now they were on to the conversation part. "Well, this is more of a work trip for me."

"Oh. You could still be having fun though."

Stupid conversational rules. She was supposed to say that she was enjoying herself even if she wasn't, not say that this was a work trip. And she *was* enjoying herself. She knew that, meant to say exactly that, and still she said things that were stuffy or borderline rude.

Okay, she'd try again. "It's nice, hiking through here." That was pretty good. Bland, which was how polite conversations were supposed to go.

"Yeah, it's always pretty right after it rains."

"Well, we need it."

Silence fell again. It seemed that her answer wasn't enough to keep the conversation game going. What had they talked about on their date? Books, movies, and music— he was into West Coast rap from the '90s, which had surprised her. What else?

Jax rubbed against her calf as she thought and she glanced down at him. His wise, mismatched eyes were somehow inquisitive and comforting all at once.

Conversation. She could do this.

"Why did you become a firefighter?" It was a question she'd always wanted to ask; what was the appeal of running into burning buildings? Was it all machismo? And if it was about helping others, well, there were plenty of other jobs that did that too. Why firefighting in particular?

She had enough presence of mind not to ask all that.

"Why?" He paused halfway up an incline, his chest working as his lungs fueled that beautiful body of his. "I don't think anyone's asked me that since my parents."

From his tone, she suspected the news hadn't gone over well. "They didn't approve?"

"My siblings all chose proper careers—I'm the youngest —and then here comes me, wanting to choose a career that wasn't..." His jaw worked as he searched for the word. "It was respectable, yeah, but it just wasn't respectable enough I guess."

"You have siblings?"

"Three. Two sisters and a brother. My brother's a lawyer in Austin, one of my sisters is a programmer in Seattle, and my other sister is in LA. She's an architect. And they all have kids, which my parents love. Being grandparents is pretty much the best thing ever for them." There was a defensive edge to his voice when he described his siblings' careers, as if he expected her to demand why he wasn't doing something similar.

"Are your parents pressuring you to settle down?"

He laughed. "Sounds like you have those kinds of parents too. Yeah, but it's not so bad. They were going to retire to Taiwan, but then Nick, my first nephew, showed up and that idea got dropped real fast."

"Did you grow up in Taiwan?"

"Um, I'd say half and half. We spent part of my childhood here, part there. I went to an American school, so it wasn't such a culture shock."

"Oh." She couldn't quite imagine such an international childhood. She'd had quite the culture shock herself when she'd left Cabrillo for college.

"Do you have any siblings?" he asked.

"A sister. She works at the resort as the wedding planner." Ofelia was like Bea; she lived for details and nothing was more detailed than a wedding. Fee was also deeply unromantic, which made her choice of careers a little surprising. Bea was closer to her cousin Lil than she was to Fee and had never really plumbed her sister's need to do something so antithetical to her nature.

"Oh yeah, the family business." Russ probably knew all about it from Luke, who ran the resort. "How did you escape it?"

"I didn't really." Her leaving Cabrillo had nothing to do with wanting to escape—she wasn't a small-town girl yearning for the big lights of the city. She still liked her small town—it just didn't happen to have a research university. "I worked at the ranch as a teenager. And of course I rode and showed and all that."

"Showed? Like that fancy jumping stuff they do?"

She snorted. "No. I rode Western pleasure. I won reserve youth champion one year too."

"What?" He stopped. "I don't believe it. Do you have pictures?"

She pulled out her phone and called up one of her mother's online photo albums. No one ever believed her, so she'd been through this song and dance before. "Here."

He looked over the picture and then whistled. "Still looks pretty fancy."

Bea understood—she and the horse had both been polished and brushed to a high sheen. "Fancy, maybe. But no jumping."

He handed the phone back with a smile. "Do you still do it?"

"No time." Which was a dull ache in her middle at times, the loss of her horses. Maybe once she had tenure she could start again.

Russ wasn't put off by the *no time* excuse. "You could find the time—"

"Wait." They weren't going off on another tangent about her. "You never said why you became a firefighter."

"Didn't I?"

He was prevaricating. Maybe because he was ashamed of the answer. Maybe it *was* all about the machismo. "No, you didn't. And you know you didn't. You took a tangent about your parents and then one about me."

"I like tangents, especially if they end in interesting pictures of you."

A pleasant shiver trickled down her spine. *Stop it.* "And there you go again."

"Okay, I became a firefighter because of Superman." He started off again with no further elaboration.

She frowned at his back. That... was not the answer she'd been expecting. "Really?"

"Yeah, when I was little I got obsessed with him. Collected all the comics, the figures, the movies—anything I could get my hands on."

"You actually do look a little like Dean Cain, you know."

He tossed her a dazzling smile, better than Dean Cain could have done. "That's the best compliment I've ever gotten."

Okay, now he was laying it on too thick. She rolled her hand at him. "Back to Superman, please."

"Anyway, I thought it was just a phase. Something to hang on to as I transitioned back to living in America."

She wondered if he knew how much he gave away with that phrase—how it put holes in his easy assurance that his international childhood had been without bumps.

"But in college..." His gaze went distant as he remembered. "It was junior year, Advanced Fluid Dynamics. I was majoring in engineering."

Wow. Not even she'd had to tackle fluid dynamics. Biology didn't require stuff like that.

"One of the other students had a heart attack," he went on. "Out of nowhere. And I just stood there, helpless. All I could do was cradle her head and tell her everything would be okay. Then the firefighters crashed in and saved her." Admiration swelled the words. "I realized then, that's what I wanted to do. I wanted to save people. Just like my idol from childhood had always done."

"Hmm. Engineering saves lives too." But for all her jokes, it was pretty noble what he'd done. Someone else might have only resolved to take a CPR class or something... but he'd chosen an entire career.

"I guess so, but it's not as exciting."

She had to give him that, although it wasn't the kind of excitement most people craved. And she sensed he was little embarrassed about it. So she used some of her few conversational skills to change the subject. "Speaking of exciting, isn't Superman the least exciting superhero? After Aquaman, of course."

He sent her a mock-wounded look. "What? Everyone loves Superman."

"Lex Luthor doesn't."

The mock-wounded expression transformed into real shock. "The man's a criminal mastermind and a supervillain."

She kept her giggles stuck in her throat since she had a little more teasing to do. "Batman doesn't like Superman, and he's not a supervillain."

He sputtered. "Batman is a humorless prick. He doesn't like anyone."

She laughed, unable to keep it in. Wow, bantering with him was fun. "Now I know what can set you off. Are you as obsessed with Superman as when you were a kid?"

"I read the comics. And collect what I can."

A nonanswer she saw right through. "So you are."

"Okay, yes." He shrugged in exasperation, but he was smiling. "There isn't anything you're obsessed with? Like *Star Trek*?"

Not this again. "Not all scientists are into nerd culture. Most of us watch and enjoy the same stuff everyone else does. Like *Game of Thrones*." You couldn't get more mainstream than dragons and beheadings and ice zombies.

"Oh." The triumph ringing in Russ's voice had Jax

coming to sharp attention. "Oh, from the way you said that, you're more than into *Game of Thrones*."

Now it was her turn to squirm. "I mean, I've read the books." *Three times.* Perfectly normal.

"What are the words of House Baratheon?"

"*Ours is the Fury*." She shook her head when he might have pounced. "Anyone could have known that."

"Okay, House Dayne?"

"Oh, we don't know that yet since that's probably a major plot point..." She halted at the smug look on his face. *Damn it.* It was hard to act mock-superior to a superhero's fandom when you'd been caught with your hand in the cookie jar of a pseudo-medieval fantasy fandom.

"We all have the things we get obsessive about," she said, trying to recover her dignity. "And you caught me—I'm obsessed with *Game of Thrones*."

They came to a flat spot amongst the rocks they'd been scrambling over, the trees and chamisal clearing before them. And—

She gasped, all thoughts of dragons and zombies chased away by what was before her. "I've never seen this view from here."

Before them the great Mojave Desert spread out. Palm Springs was a well-organized blight amid the barrenness of the desert. The mountains to their east molded the landscape below into the Coachella Valley, cradling the valley with craggy arms. It was an amazing, breath-stealing sight.

"I've seen this from the top of the tramway, but never from within the Wilderness Area." She wanted to reach for his hand, to share this moment with him, but curled her fingers into her palms instead. "It's amazing. People think the desert is just sand and cactus and nothing else, but I think it's gorgeous."

"Me too. All of it." The reverence in his voice resonated through her. "We're lucky to live here."

"Yes, we are." Just as reverent as he'd been.

They stared for several moments longer, soaking in the view and their position high above the world.

Finally Russ said reluctantly, "We'd better move on. We still have a lot of trail to cover. From here, we head up the mountain. We might be at your plants by the end of the day."

"Really?" She didn't want to leave this view any more than he did, but she did want her plants.

"Maybe. Come on."

If the route earlier had been hard, this one was plain exhausting. When they weren't marching straight up through untamed brush, they were climbing over boulders yet again. She reeked of sage, leaves were stuck in her hair, and sweat was dripping down her back.

And yet she was having fun. Just like he'd told her to. Sweaty, exhausting, muscle-tingling joy.

They came to a particularly tricky-looking boulder with a large fissure down the face of it, and she watched, trying to figure out how she was going to manage, as he climbed.

"Need a hand?" he asked from the top, reaching for her.

She shook her head. While he was no doubt strong enough to haul her up bodily, he'd climbed it and so could she. Also, she didn't want to grab his hand, not when the effect of the view of the valley below was so fresh.

This was a work trip after all.

She put her hands on the edge of the rock, found a grip, and set her toes into a notch. She pulled herself up, set her other foot higher, searching for another notch. She found one, dug her toes deep, and pushed.

It was hard work but manageable. She didn't need—

Her foot slipped out from the rock, and she banged hard against the surface. Her fingertips lost hold of the edge and she fell, hitting the ground with a *whomp*. Before she could catch her breath, she was sliding back down the trail, dirt and brush scraping and slapping at her as she slid and slid and slid.

Stop. I have to stop.

But thinking it didn't make it happen, and her heart jumped sickeningly into her throat. Reaching out an arm to try to grab something only got her scraped even worse, her fingers closing on nothing as she kept falling. She landed hard on her right hip, heat and pain tearing through her skin and ripping into her muscle.

But she'd stopped. She pulled in shaky, sick breaths, trying to calm herself. God, did her leg hurt. She pushed herself up, her elbows protesting. She must have banged those too. And there was a nasty scrape on her left forearm that stung like a bastard.

But her hip... She gasped. Her pants were shredded. Blood was already soaking the fabric, and her upper right thigh looked as though it had been dragged through gravel at high speed. Which she supposed it kind of had.

Her vision went gray, her head lolling. *Shock.* No, she couldn't pass out. She fought against the darkness, trying to keep her thoughts clear, to push the blankness at the edges of her mind away.

A hand at her back. She focused on that, on centering herself in the here and now.

"Stay with me."

Was that Russ? So firm, so commanding—not like he'd sounded before. This man didn't care if you liked him. He only wanted your obedience.

"I'm..." She wanted to say that she was okay, but her

voice died before she could. Her mouth flooded with sourness and she concentrated on not vomiting. *Mustn't puke on the hot fireman.*

She giggled at that, her head rolling as she did. *Whoops.*

"Hey. Just keep breathing. Don't pass out."

She set her awareness on the solidity of his voice, used that foundation to keep from slipping into the dark. But when she did that, the pain flared high.

What had she done to her hip?

His hand left her back, and she watched as he slipped his pack from his back, pulling out a blanket and... a knife? Definitely something long and metal and gleaming.

He set a blanket behind her and leaned her back. Then he tucked another blanket around her.

"I'm not—" But suddenly she was shivering. Worse than she had been in the cold last night. Her teeth chattered hard enough to feel loose in her jaw.

Jax crawled next to her, laying himself along her good side.

What a great dog. What an awesome dog—

"I've got to cut away your pants, all right?"

Oh God. If she hadn't been lying down, the embarrassment alone would have made her faint. Yes, he'd seen her naked before, but to have him cut away that bloody fabric and deal with the mess...

"Okay." High and reedy, as if she was about to cry. Maybe she was. Fainting, crying—would any of that be worse than him cutting off her pants?

The first snip of his scissors through the fabric was loud. He moved up her leg quickly, slicing away her pants with an efficient ease.

"You really do know what you're doing."

He smiled briefly. "I'm a paramedic."

"I thought you were a firefighter." She realized she was being silly but found herself unable to do anything about it. It was like being drunk and knowing she was drunk but not being able to will herself undrunk.

She didn't like this shock business. She couldn't recommend it.

"Most of our calls are medical nowadays." He said it as if they were only chatting together. "So I'm certified as a paramedic too."

He slowly peeled the fabric from her wound, which hurt like all hell. She bit back tears and shut her eyes tight.

Don't pass out. You've done so good so far, don't ruin it.

"You okay?"

She nodded without opening her eyes.

"Tell me if you think you might faint or vomit."

Oh God, to throw up in front of him... She dragged air between her clenched teeth, trying to think of anything but how terrible she felt.

"This is going to hurt," he said, his voice firm, bracing. "I have to irrigate this."

"Ah!" She let her breath go in short, wavery puffs, the shock of the pain wrenching her back into herself. Fuck, that hurt.

Jax whined next to her, giving her some doggy sympathy. She patted him as best she could.

"Good girl," Russ was saying. "Almost done." Another wash of cold, stinging agony on her hip. "Already looking better. You're doing so good."

She focused on the murmur of his voice, the soothing words. If he said she was doing well, she must be. After all, he was the expert here. Even though she felt like she was doing terribly.

"See, I'm not questioning you at all," she said.

He didn't laugh—instead he rested the backs of his fingers on her cheek, his gaze searing into hers. "I know it hurts, babe. You're doing awesome. I'm so proud."

Okay, that wasn't shock going through her now. Or maybe it was, just a completely different kind of shock than had hit her before.

His fingers fell. "One last one."

She was ready this time—she hardly flinched at all.

"That... that wasn't so bad." But she sounded like she was half a second away from tears.

He laughed softly. "It looks like it hurts like a son of a bitch. I'm impressed that you didn't scream."

Huh. He didn't call her babe that time or touch her. Not that she wanted that. "Do people usually scream?"

"Sometimes. But the screamers—if they're being that loud, you know they're not that badly hurt. Now the quiet ones... you've got to watch them, because they'll slip right away from you without a sound."

How many people had slipped right away from him? Without thinking, she set her hand on his forearm, the muscle there taut, steely. "I'll scream if it'll make you feel better."

"You don't have to. And I don't want to hear you scream in pain." He lifted her knee and she winced. But it wasn't quite as bad as before. He began to bandage it.

"You don't want to hear me scream, period."

"That's not true." Low and rough, halfway to his *obey me* firefighter's voice.

The heat rushing through her had nothing to do with pain. Oh God, had she screamed during their one-night stand? If only she could remember beyond "awesome sexy times."

"Did I...?"

He looked up at her, his dark brown eyes hot, intense. "Yes. It was amazing."

Oh God. *Oh God.* Her mouth fell open, but no apology came out. She wasn't a screamer. She didn't do that.

Except she had and she *didn't remember it.*

"Don't be embarrassed." Anger serrated the edge of his words. "I loved it."

That just made it worse. She put a hand over her face. Of all the people to lead her on this trip... What a disaster. If she didn't need this plant, she'd head right back down this mountain. Right after she cried her heart out.

But she did need this plant. More than anything. She dropped her hand, forced herself to face him. "Could you look in my pack for some pants, please?" she asked, all distant politeness. She wasn't going to talk about the screaming. If she pretended it hadn't happened, she might recover a hint of dignity.

"Sure." But he didn't sound happy about it. Jax followed his master, sending her one last worried look as he moved away.

While Russ rummaged in her pack, she took stock of herself. Battered, embarrassed, and with no nightshade penstemon. Oh, and pantsless. She ran her hands through her hair, fixing it as best she could, dirt and gravel raining from her scalp. Great. She wouldn't be able to get all that out until she found a shower, two days from now.

She forced her lungs to fill. It was all right. He'd give her some pants, she'd get dressed, and they could get on with this hike from hell. The trip was still salvageable.

He handed her a pair of pants, but when she tried to take them from him, he pulled them away again.

"Hang on. I've got to help you."

She pushed herself up. "No, it's—" But when she tried to put weight on her leg, it failed her.

Russ caught her. "Easy. I've got you."

That's what she was afraid of. His arms were solid, strong, and he somehow managed to be several inches taller than her. Most men couldn't do that—how had he done it?

That made no sense. She must still be woozy.

With his help, she got into her pants, painfully aware of how close his face was to her thighs and crotch. So, so painfully aware.

But soon enough she had her pants on and both feet on the ground, although he didn't let go of her.

"Think you can stand?" He clearly didn't think she could.

She nodded and he slowly released her. Her legs held. *Thank you, Jesus.* She put up an arm to ask for some distance between them. "I'm fine. Really."

But she wasn't so certain the leg holding her up would keep doing so when she started walking. Only one way to find out. She started for her pack, testing out her leg. It hurt, but she could use it.

"We're not too far from the trailhead," Russ said. "We should be able to make it back to the cars by dark."

She stopped dead as she went for her pack. "Wait? What? We're not leaving."

The cold command came back into his expression. "Yes. We are. That's a hell of a scrape you've got on your leg. Come tomorrow, with all the bruising, you'll be lucky to be able to walk."

"No, we've got to go on." She didn't bother to keep the desperation from her voice. "I'll be fine."

"Okay, you can drop the Wonder Woman act. Seriously."

"It's not an act." And he was the one obsessed with

Wonder Woman. "If I say I can go on, I can." She pulled her pack back on, setting her chin at a hard angle.

He looked doubtful.

She crossed her arms. "I'm not leaving without my penstemon." She could do cold command herself.

"We could come later."

"No! It has to be the blooms. If we try again, it might be too late." She took one step, then another, away from him, inching back toward their trail.

"It's only a plant. I don't want you to get hurt."

Too late for that. "It's not only a plant. I told you a lot of people's careers are riding on this, not just mine." He still didn't looked convinced, so she went for the nuclear option. "I won't leave. You can't make me."

Exactly like a spoiled toddler, but she was not leaving. Not for one banged-up leg, which hardly even hurt. She put more weight on it and winced. Okay, it really hurt a lot, but she could walk.

He studied her for long moments, all the friendliness gone from his expression. He didn't look as if he cared whether she liked him—and she liked him all the more for it in this moment. Which was perverse.

"I actually could make you." A rough growl. "Ever heard of a fireman's lift?"

His arms flexed and her mouth went dry. Because he very much looked like he could carry her all the way back to the trailhead. And she found him attractive enough to wonder for a moment what that might feel like.

"At least let me try. Please." Begging, but that's exactly what she was willing to do. "You're assuming I can't make it without any evidence."

Reason. Men loved it when you appealed to their reason.

His lips pursed. "So you're proposing we hike farther

into the wilderness, find out you can't make it, and then we have to hike that much farther back out?"

Okay, that did sound dumb. How to reframe her argument? "But if I can make it, we'll be that much closer to where we need to be." She put on her imperious-professor look, the one she used when someone asked a question in a seminar meant to make her look bad and the questioner look smart.

It didn't work on him. "If you can't make it, my argument still stands."

He was right, damn it. "We don't know that I can't make it. Shouldn't we test your theory?"

"An experiment?"

"Exactly." To prove the evidence was in favor of her theory, she put her weight on her bad leg. All her weight. The leg held, even though her teeth were gritted hard enough that she could hear the enamel grinding away.

He smiled, which made his handsomeness go from smoldering to smoking. "All right. You've made it clear you're pigheaded enough to do this. Let's see if we can make it to our next campsite by dusk."

Pigheaded wasn't very nice, but she supposed it fit in this case. "Let's go then."

"Wait." He motioned to her backpack. "There's no way you can carry that with your leg. Give it here." He somehow hefted both packs onto his back, easy as pie. He must spend so much time in the gym, those thigh muscles bulging as he did squats, his ass coming into sharp relief as he deadlifted...

"What is it?" He looked behind him as if to find what she'd been staring at.

How much do you squat?

She didn't even mean to ask that, but when he laughed and said, "Three fifty," she was glad she had.

"And deadlift?"

"Four hundred."

He started off and she followed behind, admiring his legs again, her own leg dragging a bit.

"Like, that's your normal workout?"

"Jesus, no. That's a one-rep max." Ah, so he'd told her that to impress her. "Why? Do you lift?"

She did, although she'd never admit the main reason why—the weight lifters were in the weight room. If she had to be sweaty and sore, might as well have some eye candy to look at. "Clearly not like you do."

"Enjoy the view." His smile made her feel as if steam were rising from her. "We've got a ways to go."

She planned to, if only to take her mind off the pain now building in her leg.

Chapter 4

RUSS PACKED AWAY THE REMAINS of his lunch, tossing a cracker to Jax as he did. The dog caught it with a lightning-fast snap of his jaws. Damn, that always impressed Russ, how fast that dog was.

He pulled out his water bottle and took a swig, using the motion to study Bea. She was propped against a rock, her injured leg stretched out before her, her head drooping as she nibbled at her own lunch.

"You okay?" Although he already knew what she'd answer.

"I'm fine."

There it was, exactly what he'd expected. She didn't look fine, and it killed him that she was so clearly uncomfortable. He ought to have hauled her back despite her little tantrum—he hadn't been lying when he'd said he could. It might have even been fun, having her draped over his shoulder, her ass swinging in the air. He could even give it a few taps when he felt like it.

And when they arrived at the trailhead and he unslung

her from his shoulder, she'd be more pissed off than a cat tossed into a bathtub.

Yeah, the fireman's lift was out as a solution. He dusted off his hands and crossed over to her. "I should probably check your wound. But first—" He reached into one of the pockets of his cargo shorts and handed her a wrapped treat.

She turned it over in her hands. "What is it?"

Well, that proved she couldn't read Mandarin. But no one was perfect. "It's a moon cake. My mom picks them up by the hundreds in Taiwan and has them shipped here. Every time she sees me, she gives me a boxful."

"Oh. The wrapping is very pretty."

It was—the foil was a dusky rose color with the lettering in a deep plum. "Try it," he urged. "It'll help you feel better."

"I feel fine." She tore open the wrapper. "And sugar has no analgesic properties."

"Not true," he said. "I keep Ho Hos on me for any kids we meet on a call. They work like magic."

She took a nibble. "Mmm. This is much better than a Ho Ho."

"Yeah, most things are."

A strangely furtive look came over her face. "Yeah, Ho Hos are no good."

Realization dawned. "You actually like Ho Hos, don't you?"

"No." Her eyes went shifty. "Well, not that much."

"Come on, there's more."

"Okay, I have this... thing for Ding Dongs. Like, I always have to have some on hand. And I usually have one every day."

He whistled. "Ding Dongs?" He never would have thought Bea had it in her to eat something named "dong" every day. At least not the Bea he'd met on this trip. Maybe the Bea from their date...

She took the last bite of cake. "Yes, well, I didn't name them. And I don't understand why I like them so much. They're really just chocolate-flavored sugar and chemicals."

"But don't they also have the chocolate coating? Maybe that's it."

He'd meant it as a tweak, but a thoughtful look came over her face. "Maybe that is it. I never considered that before. I do really like the chocolate coating."

A corner of his mouth ticked up. Only Bea would seriously consider the question of why she liked Ding Dongs so much. "How's the leg?"

She rose and tucked the cake wrapper into her backpack. "Better, thank you."

That was a different story from "fine." But if she was feeling better, that was good. She was carrying a decent amount of weight on it with some stiffness, but not much. He didn't linger on her ass as he checked her leg—at least not much.

Now to ease her into his next awkward request—

His phone buzzed in his pocket, letting him know he had a text message. He fished it out and shook his head when he saw it.

You didn't call this morning. Are you alive? Mom

He moved off to give himself some privacy, his fingers flying as he wrote back: *Woke up too late to call.*

His mother was an investment banker and was usually at her desk before sunup.

You can still call.

I don't want to interrupt. And clearly I'm alive.

Smart-mouth. How is this girl you're with?

Mooommm! She's a client.

I heard from your sister she's a professor.

Russ was going to kill Stacy when he saw her next. *And maybe she's married,* he texted back.

She's not.

How did his mother know? She had more than eyes in the back of her head—sometimes he thought his mom might be psychic.

Okay, she's not.

He paused, trying to think of what to say next. Because he *was* interested in Bea, very much so—but she clearly had no interest in him. And he couldn't quite say why. Their failed date—or rather, not-so-failed date—shouldn't have been that much of a stumbling block.

Perhaps he ought to turn this back on his mom. With love, of course.

Maybe I'll come back with a new daughter-in-law for you. He grinned evilly as he typed it.

It took several moments for her message to come back, moments he imagined her furiously typing and deleting multiple replies.

Don't agree to anything until we meet her.

Meaning that his mom did want to meet her. Suddenly it wasn't funny anymore.

Look, she's nice, and smart—he left off superhot for obvious reasons—*but we wouldn't suit.*

There. That was true and also politic.

I am sighing, my son. Very heavily.

You are not. You just like to pretend you're desperate for me to get married so you can hold your head high when you visit your friends.

Another long pause where he imagined her trying not to smile.

Please do not tell anyone, she finally replied.

Your secret is safe with me.

You keep yourself safe on this hiking trip. And call me tomorrow morning so I know you're alive.

I will if I can get a signal. I love you.

I love you too.

He slipped his phone back into his pocket and turned toward Bea. She was on the phone herself, her voice thin and high with anxiety.

"Lil, if you need me to come back—" She suddenly shut her mouth tight, listening intently. "Okay, but I'm worried about you."

Russ's instincts went on high alert.

"You say not to worry," she went on, "but you're clearly very upset." She gave a negative swipe of her hand. "No, it's not just the pregnancy."

Huh. Lil was Luke's sister. Russ had met her a few times and she'd seemed pretty cool. But Luke hadn't said anything about his sister being pregnant.

"If you don't want to be around him anymore, I'll be home so fast—" Again, she bit off the rest. "No, I can get the plants another time."

Interesting. She'd told him she couldn't. He realized he was staring, but he couldn't look away from her distress.

"If you're sure."

Russ recognized that one—the way to end a conversation when you hadn't won but didn't want to continue the fight.

"Okay, I love you too. And call me if you need anything." Bea hung up and stared at the ground as the phone hung limply from her hand.

"Everything okay?" he asked. He took a step toward her, but just the one.

"I'm fine."

"Yeah, I got that." He decided to throw caution to the wind. "You're willing to abandon this whole trip for your cousin, but not because you're injured?"

Bea's glare was sharp enough to slice a tin can. "She's pregnant and trying to work things out with the father, but..." Her expression softened. "It's not going well."

Russ's instincts went into overdrive. "Is he hurting her?"

"No. Nothing like that." Bea frowned as she tried to explain. "She's just... I've never seen her this upset."

"Do you want to go back anyway?" He couldn't quite understand what was going on with Lil, but Bea was upset herself. He wanted to fix this for her.

Bea's mouth pursed as she studied the ground. "No. Lil said she didn't need me. And I need this plant."

Back to the plant. Always back to that. And speaking of need... "I should look at your leg."

She went white. "Is that necessary?"

"I want to see if the bleeding stopped."

"Fine," she bit off.

That made him feel like shit, but he went to help her pull off her pants anyway. She leaned against him, her arms reluctantly sliding around his shoulders, their heads bent together. He let her unbutton her pants but put his own hands around the waistband. "Ready?" he asked. "It might hurt some."

She nodded and he gently worked the pants down to her knees, enough to see the bandage covering her thigh. A few pink splotches had worked their way through the gauze, but otherwise it looked good.

The rest of her did too. He was an asshole for doing it, but he took his time taking all of her in. Smooth thighs, the scent of her soap rising from her skin—tea rose, which was just old-fashioned enough to delight him—the tiny flowers printed on her blue panties, and the mound of her sex, begging for the cup of his palm.

He couldn't help it—he set a hand to her hip as he crouched before her, her arms braced against his shoulders, and he looked up.

Her eyes were half-closed, her lips parted... He knew that look. He'd seen it before, in his bed, as she'd tossed with pleasure beneath his hands.

He slowly rose, cupped her jaw with his hand. Her eyes went wide.

"Tell me no," he ordered, because she had to say yes. She couldn't get away—her jeans were trapping her—but she couldn't cry foul on this if she said yes.

"I can't," she whispered.

"Not good enough. You've got to tell me no. Or yes. Pick one."

"I—"

"Don't tell me *I can't*. You can do anything you set your mind to, and we both know it. Pick, Beatriz. You're not drunk, I'm not bought—this is just you and me. No excuses."

A sharp inhale. She was frightened. Of him, of her desire—he couldn't say. Her chin came forward, too enticing to be a jut, and she said, "Yes."

He captured her mouth, just as he'd wanted to do since he'd seen her climb out of her car at the trailhead. She tasted sweet and bright and intoxicating. He slid a hand into the silk of her hair, anchoring her as he nudged her mouth open.

The moment her tongue touched his was electric, a spark arcing between them to sizzle through his veins. He'd gladly let the desire between them burn out each and every one of his neurons—she was worth it.

She bobbled, moaning a little into his mouth. He wrapped his free arm around her waist. "I've got you," he murmured into her ear. "I've got you."

"Russ."

God, the shaky, needy way she got that out—it hit him hard. "Yeah, babe?" He'd give her anything she wanted. Everything she wanted.

She put her face away from his. "My pants... I can't."

She didn't want to go further—*she wanted him to pull up her pants.* Shit.

He swallowed hard, taking a moment to get himself together. He'd given her a scorching kiss, and she was worried about her pants. So much for her being as carried away as he was.

He eased her pants back up and fastened them for her. When he glanced at her face, she was breathing funny and her cheeks were pink.

She wanted this, but she didn't want to want it, not even when he tried to force a straight answer from her. He closed his eyes for half a moment. What else should he have expected?

"Are you okay?" He didn't mean to sound so gruff, but he felt like he was always asking her that.

And he was a touch frustrated after that kiss.

"I'm fine." And he felt like she was always answering that.

"Let's go get your plant then."

She didn't answer, just pulled her pack on and trudged off, looking as grim as he felt.

HER LEG WAS KILLING HER.

She'd never admit that to him, and she could tell her repetition of "I'm fine" was grating on him, but it really, really hurt. She could walk, so thank God for small mercies, but she was definitely slower than before no matter how hard she pushed.

This stupid trip. That stupid date. Her stupid leg.

She frowned at the back of Russ's head. And that stupid, hot kiss. Why did he have to be so good with his mouth?

Just you and me. No excuses. I've got you. The memory was making her melt inside. It would be so easy to fall into the fantasy that he was a real-life superhero, come to save her sex life.

But life wasn't like that. Superman wasn't even human—he was an alien, for Pete's sake. Russ was most definitely human, albeit a superior specimen. He was a superhuman kisser, that was for sure. A lot of men might be sloppy or slobbery, but his mouth had been slick and sleek, with enough wet heat to tantalize her. He'd tasted of something spicy, almost cinnamony. How had he managed that?

She really ought to stop pondering that kiss. The memories were turning her to jelly once more—needy, sex-hungry jelly.

Jax nudged her hand with his nose, and she absently petted him between each lumbering step on her bad leg. The dog seemed to have an uncanny ability to sense when she was upset.

"Doing okay?"

Man, was she sick of that question. Probably about as sick as he was of asking it.

"I'm fine." She hadn't said anything other than those two words the entire afternoon. She'd thought the lack of conversation would be a relief, but she found herself actually wanting to speak. Bursting with the desire almost.

A pretty sprig of lupine—she'd wanted to point that out to him. The difficulty of the climb—she'd wanted to express her admiration at how easily he was handling it. The awesomeness of his dog—she'd wanted to share that with him, although he probably already knew.

Bea, a person who avoided social conversations as much as she could, had found someone she actually wanted to make small talk with. And there was a metric shit ton of baggage between them.

He glanced back at her and then did a double take. "What'd I do?"

Been utterly awesome, you big jerk wad.

"Nothing. This is just how I look." *Resting bitch face to the rescue.*

"No, you're pissed about something."

"You know, you keep making these assumptions about me like you know me." Never mind that he was crazy good at reading her—he *didn't* know her.

"Yeah, but most of my assumptions turn out to be true," he said. How casually assured a man could be—Bea didn't think she could put that much easy arrogance into her voice. "Which maybe makes them more than assumptions."

She wasn't touching that one. "I'm not pissed. I promise."

"Is it about the kiss?"

She hadn't been expecting that one. "Yes, I have been thinking about it."

"You think too much."

"Oh, I should just fall into your arms instead?" He'd like that, wouldn't he?

"You did it once and you liked it. I know you did—not an assumption. Your screams that night proved it."

Jesus. He really was a jerk wad. "You're determined to

embarrass me at every turn!"

"No, you're determined to be embarrassed." So unfazed, this guy. "Which is different."

What an infuriating, smug, arrogant horse's ass. Although that might be an insult to horses' asses, which at least produced manure.

"I don't want to talk about this anymore," she bit out.

"There's a surprise."

She didn't see it, but she knew, just knew, he was rolling his eyes.

"You're only here to guide me to my plants, not compile a psych profile," she said. "Which you're not very good at."

"Then why are you so angry?"

"Because my leg is killing me!" *And you won't stop bringing up that date.*

"Huh. And you said you were fine."

Why did he keep asking how she was if he wasn't going to believe her answers? Jax nudged her again, and she gave him a quick pet. "Are you going to drag me back down the mountain now?"

"No. You're keeping up, and while it might take another day, you'll make it if you can sustain this pace."

"Oh." Well, she hadn't been expecting that after her confession that her leg hurt.

"But see," he said in an irritatingly arch tone, "you admitted that you're in pain, and I didn't force you to quit. You can admit your weaknesses—I won't use them against you."

"I didn't..." But she had. She'd thought all along that this was a battle and he was going to poke at her soft bits and sneer as she curled up like a hedgehog. Perhaps that wasn't it at all though. She gathered herself, pondered what to say next. "I'm sorry."

Huh. That had not been on her list of possible answers, so where had it come from?

"You don't have to be sorry. Just... just don't assume I'm here to hurt or humiliate you. I'm here to protect you."

Shades of Superman there. But she wasn't a comic book girlfriend, conveniently out of frame when she wasn't needed—she was a complicated, difficult person in her own right.

A clearing was coming into sight, an almost unnaturally regular square of bright green. She frowned as she peered at it. What kind of plant was growing there and in such abundance? There was a weird smell too, a dank kind of smell.

"I don't expect you—" But the rest of what she was about to say was lost as she blinked at a length of black pipe snaking toward the plants. *Irrigation hose? What the...?*

Russ had stopped dead too. "Is this what I think it is?"

She took a deep breath, the musty smell filling her lungs. Brighter, less intense than usual, but she recognized it. "Marijuana."

Her heart kicked into double time. They had stumbled on an illegal field of pot. Just sitting here in the middle of nowhere. And with the irrigation running to it, clearly it was someone's.

"Shit. Shit, shit, shit." Russ's hand was clenching and unclenching, and Jax whined up at him. "I fucking hate this shit. Assholes. To fuck up the wilderness area with this shit —not to mention the fire danger..."

She gaped at him. If she hadn't seen it with her own eyes, she'd have never thought it possible—Russ could get really, really *angry*.

He pulled his phone out of his pocket. "I've got to call this in. Sorry about your plants." That last was tossed off as almost an afterthought.

Her stomach bounced. "Wait—what about my plants?"

He lowered the phone. "I've got to call in the authorities so they can take care of this. We can't make it to the penstemon now."

No. No, that was not happening. "Why do you need to call it in this very moment?"

"Are you serious? Of course I have to call it in." But he didn't raise the phone.

"Yes, but not *now*. We can go get the nightshade penstemon, then alert the authorities on our way back."

He blinked at her. "You are unbelievable. We can come back in a couple of weeks when your leg is healed—"

"No! It has to be the blooms. We wait a week and it will be another year before I can get them."

"I'm not breaking the law for you." He put the phone to his ear.

She caught his wrist. "I'm not asking you to break the law. This field isn't going anywhere. And clearly"—she gestured to the lush growth—"it's been here a while. What does one day matter to you?" She tightened her grip on his wrist, the tendons steely beneath her fingers. "Because it matters the world to me. And my lab. And maybe even medical science."

He lowered the phone, but his jaw was tight. She kept her fingers wrapped around his wrist, the strength of it seeming to pulse through her own veins.

When he kept quiet, she went on, "There's seven people all relying on me and this plant. My entire career is wrapped up in this trip."

Her entire identity, really. If she weren't a scientist, what would she be? It was all or nothing in academia, and if she was denied tenure, she'd be nothing.

The bones of his wrist seemed to harden beneath her

fingers, and she realized she was holding him much, much too tightly. She eased her grip but didn't let go.

He was struggling with his decision—the muscle in his jaw twitched with each thought sparking through his mind. He wanted to be the hero here—Superman would call it in right away.

But he had a... a *tenderness* for her. She didn't understand it, wasn't certain if it was only some weird offshoot of his need to have everyone like him, but it was there.

She had to push him into that tenderness. And she'd do it by admitting her weakness.

"Please," she said, letting her voice break with her need. "Please. You know what this means to me."

He averted his face, the hand she was holding clenching into a fist. Damn. It wasn't working.

And then: "Fine."

So brusque and bitten off, she didn't recognize it as agreement at first.

"We'll get my plant first?"

He turned back to her, his expression a mix of resignation and frustration. "I hate the idea, but yeah. We'll get your plant first and call this in on our way back."

She grinned up at him and squeezed his wrist. A slow smile took hold of his mouth, and that lightning spark passed between them, the one that heralded the thunder of a kiss.

Uh-oh. She dropped his hand and stepped away, blinking to try to clear her head. They'd just been fighting and now she wanted to jump him. God, but he mixed her up good.

"Thank you," she got out. "Everything will work out. You'll see."

"Will it?" Soft. Kind of sad.

"Yes." She kept her gaze averted, afraid of what she might see in his eyes.

"Let's keep on then. The sooner we can get this plant, the sooner my mind will be at ease."

Hers too.

They walked another half hour or so in a sharp-edged silence. Russ was not happy about this, his unease a force field surrounding him.

Bea, even though she'd gotten her way, wasn't any happier. That field of pot rubbed at the edges of her conscience. She didn't really care that someone was growing pot—meth was a much worse scourge here—but to do it in the middle of the wilderness area was too much. Russ was right: it was a danger to the preserve.

But one more day shouldn't hurt. After all, they'd found it and were going to do something about it—they were doing the right thing, if only a day later than they might have. Russ would still play Superman like he wanted to.

Bea was so absorbed in arguing with herself she didn't notice the other woman until they were almost upon her.

The woman was tall and thin, with dishwater-blond hair tucked into a messy bun, her shirt and pants the same dull brown as her hair. She carried no pack, but her weather-tanned skin said that she spent a fair amount of time outdoors.

Had Bea seen her out and about in town, she might have said the woman was a hippie or at least very crunchy. The kind who shopped at a food co-op, drove a thirty-year-old Subaru, and could preserve food like nobody's business.

Bea would have said that in town, but not here.

Because the woman was carrying a gun.

Chapter 5

THEY'D FOUND THE OWNER OF the pot field.

And she was holding a shotgun.

Loosely holding a shotgun, Russ amended, but still holding it. He spread his fingers and half lifted his hands, assuming a nonthreatening position. "Morning," he called out to her as if she were any other hiker on the trail.

"Morning," she said. Not really friendly, but she hadn't raised the gun.

Russ unobtrusively put himself in front of Bea, Jax crowding close to her side. "Are you out hunting?"

He knew damn well she wasn't, not in the wilderness area, but he put a heaping helping of *hey-brah-surfer-dude* in his voice so she would think he was an idiot.

Bea kept quiet, thank God.

The woman snorted. "No. What are you doing?"

"Oh man." Russ shook his head and chuckled. "You won't believe it, but we were camping and my wife banged the shit out of her leg. So now we're headed back to the trailhead." He made his tone light, as if they were sharing this story over a beer. But he kept Bea tucked behind him.

The woman halted about ten feet away, an unfriendly distance. "You're going the wrong way."

"We are?" He almost smacked his forehead but decided that would be too much. "Man, the map on the phone told us to go this way."

"You should be heading the other way." She pointed with her free hand. "Due southeast."

"Thanks. I don't know what we would have done without you." Russ gave her a smile that didn't acknowledge the gun in her hand. And although his every instinct screamed not to, he turned his back on her and said to Bea, "Come on, babe. We've got to backtrack."

Bea's eyes were wide, her cheeks pale, but she said with incredible poise, "Okay. Thank you, ma'am."

Bea began walking back the way they'd come, back toward that goddamn pot field that was going to get them killed. He ought to have called the moment he'd seen it and let the sheriffs confront this woman, but he'd let Bea's pleading eyes convince him not to. Superman probably never listened to his dick and never found himself in shit like this.

Russ started after her, putting a hand at her elbow, trying to ignore the weight of that gun on his back. Bea gave him a quick, frightened glance, and he did his best to reassure her only with his eyes. Her limp was worse, and she brushed against him heavily with each agonized step.

Bea couldn't give up now—they had to get out of here and quick.

"I don't think your wife is going to make it."

Shit. They both went still. The hair on Russ's neck prickled, but he kept his expression neutral as he turned back to the woman. "Sorry?"

"Your wife's leg." The woman gestured to Bea. "She can

hardly walk." There was a hint of accusation there, as if it were Russ's fault Bea had the audacity to limp.

"I'm fine," Bea said. "Really, I am." Her voice was thin and high.

Don't give us away. Be strong just a little longer.

"You sound like you're in pain." The woman gestured them forward. "You should come back to my camp. Jilly has a salve for bruising. It'll help you."

Oh shit. Oh shit, shit, shit. Camp? They had a camp? With more than just her?

The surfer dude Russ was supposed to be would just go merrily along with this woman's suggestion. The firefighter in Russ was screaming *hell no.*

"Babe?" He gave Bea a look. "Do you want to do that?" *Play along. I'm good cop—now you be the bad cop.*

She got the message. "I'm okay, really." The strength had returned to her voice. "But I appreciate it." Firmly dismissive.

That was his girl. He gave her elbow a squeeze of appreciation.

"We don't bite," the woman said.

You don't need to—you're holding a gun.

"You sure, babe?" he asked Bea. He wanted to leave this woman without another word, but he also didn't want to raise her suspicions.

"I... I don't know." Bea's gaze flicked toward the gun, then back to Russ, naked pleading there.

Oh, honey. Russ was trained for this sort of thing—sometimes you ran into someone carrying a gun on a call—but she wasn't. And he wasn't quite sure how to get them out of this, not without endangering her.

If he were on his own, he'd probably go with the woman to find out where this illegal camp was, then he'd report both her growing operation and her camp. But Bea wasn't here for the superhero stuff.

Keep her safe. The first rule, and he'd skirted it at every opportunity. And now he was reaping the whirlwind.

"Do you think you can make it back to the car?" he asked.

Hardness crept into Bea's expression—she was reaching for bravery, and it made his heart wring out. "Of course." Slowly she put all her weight on her bad leg, lifting the good leg even.

And then she stumbled.

He caught her before she fell, her arms coming around his neck as he pulled her close to him. Her effort had been brave, but it hadn't worked—and no doubt Bea would beat herself up over it.

"It's okay," he muttered close to her ear. He wasn't certain if she heard.

"Look, if you guys want to hike out in the dark like that, whatever," the woman said. The barrel of the gun came up a few inches. "What trail are you going to take?" Coldness slithered into her tone.

She wanted to know if they might stumble onto her pot field. At least she didn't know that they'd already found it.

"I guess we should go with her," Bea said, sidestepping the trail question. "After a night's rest—and that salve—I should be perfectly able to hike out."

"Really?" He was so surprised he dropped his laid-back persona for a moment. "I mean cool. I don't want you to hurt yourself. More."

Fuck. How to get them out of this?

"Fine." The woman seemed to suddenly regret the offer. "We'll get you patched up, you can stay the night"—the sun was already halfway set—"and you can be on your way in the morning."

He knew why Bea had done that—to deflect from the woman's suspicion—and it had gotten them out of that particular mess, but now they were in a new one. There was nothing to do now though except play the ball as it lay.

"Cool. I'm Russ, by the way." He almost offered his hand and then realized the woman was too far away for a handshake. "This is Bea. And Jax."

Jax didn't wag his butt in welcome. Smart dog.

The woman nodded briefly, then started off. "I'm Ash. The camp is this way."

Russ followed her, Bea leaning heavily on him. The woman—Ash—took them down the main trail for about half a mile and then ducked onto a side trail hidden in the brush, one carved out solely by people walking down it. She said nothing as they walked, never once looked back at them. Russ couldn't get a read on her. She'd invited them to her camp, but she wasn't exactly welcoming. So why do it?

"You guys set up like a commune here?" Russ asked. He hoped she might say something about how big this place was and if anyone else might be armed—give him some clues about how to play this.

"Kind of."

Which didn't tell him anything. "They let you set up a camp here in the forest? That's pretty cool."

Ash slid him a glance. "No, they didn't. But we believe all land is held in common, so it doesn't matter what they allow or don't."

"Oh." So these weren't run-of-the-mill marijuana farmers—they were idealists. Which might make them even more dangerous.

Ash looked back at Bea, who was leaning heavily on

Russ as he led them both into deeper trouble. "We're almost there," Ash said. Then she looked at Jax. "We've got a lot of dogs in the camp—you should maybe keep him away from them. They don't like new dogs coming in."

Great. Now Jax was in danger too.

"Sure. I'll keep him close to me."

Jax tilted his head inquiringly. Russ wanted to give him a reassuring pat, but his hands were full keeping Bea going.

"We have a spare tent you two can use," Ash said. "You should keep him there."

Bea flinched against him, the ripples from it shivering through him. They'd had separate tents this whole time—she wasn't happy about sharing. But they were supposed to be married.

They both had a lot to hide here. He didn't want these people to know that he knew this wilderness like the back of his hand. And he certainly didn't want them to know he was a firefighter.

"Thanks." Sometimes he was amazed at his ability to fake enthusiasm. "We've got our own, but we're happy not to have to set that one up. I'm an engineer, but it's still tricky."

Ash's expression took on a twinge of disgust. Russ couldn't blame her—not being able to set up a tent was pretty pathetic.

"I think you did fine," Bea said. She didn't quite hit *doting wife*, but Russ had to give her points for effort. Even if she were really his wife, he didn't think Bea would ever be doting.

"We're here," Ash said shortly, then pushed her way through some brush taller than even Russ and down an embankment. "Wait here so the kids can catch up the dogs." She cupped her hands around her mouth. "Put up the dogs. Now!"

They'd chosen a wash for their camp, one with cotton-woods growing tall and wide, a perfect concealment of what was going on beneath. The camp wasn't huge—maybe five tents, with a couple of picnic tables under a pop-up and a makeshift kitchen. Come winter, it would be cold and exposed—and in danger of sliding away in a hard rain—but Russ guessed they wouldn't stay that long. No, they'd break this down and haul it off somewhere warmer, maybe across the border.

A gaggle of four kids came running up to greet them. The kids, who probably ranged from about five to twelve years old, were barefoot and grimy, their clothes mismatched. But they looked happy enough.

"Did you put up the dogs?" Ash asked.

"Yes," the kids all chorused together, bouncing their way toward them.

"Hey," the tallest boy said, "who are you?"

"Give them some space," Ash ordered.

The kids pressed closer. Russ guessed they didn't see too many new people here.

"I'm Russ, and this is Bea."

"Hi," Bea said weakly even as she shrank closer to him.

"Are you going to live with us?" That from one of the girls, probably about eight or so.

He couldn't help grinning. Kids were so amazing. "No. We're just visiting."

"Visitors," the smallest boy began to chant. "Visitors, visitors, visitors!"

The other kids joined in as they ran alongside the adults.

Ash shook her head. Russ got the impression that these weren't her kids. "Come on," she said to them. "Let's get that dog put away so we can let the others loose."

"Sure."

Another woman poked her head out of a tent as they passed, younger but as weatherworn as Ash. "What's going on?"

"They're lost," Ash said. "And she's hurt. Can you get your salve?"

Ah, this must be Jilly.

"Sure thing. Nice dog."

Well, Jilly was definitely friendlier than Ash. It was strange that they hadn't seen any men. Maybe this was a women-only commune.

"How many people live here?" he asked Ash as if he were only making conversation. "You've done a lot of work."

"There's Jilly and her dad Jake, and all those are her kids. Then me."

That gave him a better idea of the camp dynamics. A camp of mostly women and kids—and they'd put together a pretty intricate marijuana grow. Russ was impressed in spite of himself.

Bea was looking around with an expression he could only call "scientific." Like she wanted to catalog and probe everything she was seeing, but at least she didn't look scared anymore.

"Will you guys be here all winter? Won't it get cold?" God, he sounded like such an idiot. But if they believed he actually was an idiot, Bea and he might get out of here alive.

"No. We never stay anywhere long. The world is wide and we're not tied to one place." Ash's voice was the warmest he'd heard from her yet. "So why shouldn't we explore it? Come winter, we'll pack all this up and head south."

"Just like a migrating bird," Bea piped up.

Russ almost laughed. Yeah, a migrating bird with a weed stash.

"Exactly," Ash said, approval lightening her expression. "You get it." She stopped in front of a two-man tent. "Here you go. Jilly's bringing the salve. Dinner's in an hour."

Wow, they were even going to feed them. This was almost friendly except for all the illegality.

"Do you need help?" He might be planning to turn them over to the authorities and break up their camp, but good manners insisted that he offer assistance.

Bea's fingers dug deep into his bicep. She probably thought he was going to leave her alone with all these kids.

"No," Ash said. "Your wife needs to rest her leg. Get that dog inside."

Ash worried about Bea, then barked at him in the same breath. Yeah, it was going to be tough to get a bead on her.

Once he'd unzipped the tent flap, he motioned Jax in. Right as the dog's furry butt was disappearing inside, Jilly came jogging up with the salve. "Here you go. Seriously, you'll heal so fast with this. And it's all-natural."

At this distance Russ could see that she was little younger than Ash—maybe five years or so. He wondered how she and Ash had ended up here. Maybe they were together.

Bea took the tin of salve with a tight smile. "Thanks." She disappeared into the tent with Jax.

Russ stared after her—poor Bea was probably at the end of her sociability. Not that he could blame her. "Dinner's in an hour, huh?" He gave them his winningest smile, sanded with a hint of dimness.

Jilly responded with a spark in her eyes that he knew all too well, having seen it so often when women found out what he did or saw him out and about in his uniform.

"Yeah." Ash wasn't impressed though. "Come on, Jilly."

As they left, Russ went in to go talk to his newly acquired "wife."

BEA DIDN'T BEGIN to shake until the tent flap had closed behind Russ, which she thought was an amazing accomplishment on her part. But once the shivers started, they shook her hard, making every muscle tight as her fear worked its way through her body.

Jesus, that woman had held a gun on them, and now they were... hostages? Or something. Bea didn't quite know. Maybe Ash didn't know they knew about the pot field. Maybe she only suspected.

Or maybe she knew and was just waiting until nightfall to murder them in their beds. Did people kill each other over pot? Weren't most potheads too laid-back to do stuff like that?

Bea wrapped her arms around herself as she tried to ponder that. The only potheads she knew were scientists, so they weren't a representative sample. Which meant there was a good chance they would end up murdered in their sleep—

"Hey." Russ set a hand on her shoulder, his voice low. "It's okay. We're safe. They don't mean to hurt us."

She just shook harder, because Russ had no idea if that was true. His hand slid down her arm and he turned her around, taking her in his arms.

"It's okay," he said softly. "I'll keep you safe. Don't be scared." He whispered that last right into her ear, and still Bea feared that Ash would somehow hear.

Jax nudged her hand, and she looked down at him.

There was such worry in his face—how did a dog manage to look so concerned? And how could that warm her heart so?

"Jax will keep you safe too," Russ said. "Trust us." His hand made lazy sweeps along her arm, lulling her in time with his words.

She wished she could. She wished she could just collapse into his arms and let all her worry sink onto his shoulders. But she wasn't built like that.

Putting a sliver of space between them, she said, "You were right: I should have let you call. And now we're trapped in a remake of *Deliverance* thanks to me."

She couldn't put quite as much sarcasm as she wanted into that, not with the whispering.

His chest shook as he laughed, the vibrations echoing through her. "*Deliverance*? It's not that bad. Encountering people with guns is part of my training—you learn who's likely to pop off." His hand slipped around to her back, their chests meeting. "And there's none of that crazed tension here. I think we really did just stumble on some hippies."

"I think you're only saying that to make me feel better." Although the slow slide of his hand along her spine *was* pretty comforting.

"Well, my gut is telling me not to worry. That and the fact that I'm about to call the sheriff."

"Oh." It hadn't even occurred to her to call for help. Which was stupid. Thank God he had a clearer head than she did. But— "What happens when the cavalry arrives?" She didn't want to be caught in the middle of some shoot-out.

"We'll call them, sneak out of here, and let the authorities deal with it."

He made it sound so easy, as if when she and Russ

melted away, the camp would simply cease to exist. "But there are kids here," she hissed, trying to keep her voice low.

"They're not going to come in with guns blazing." He went stiff though, his arm tightening around her. That thought apparently unnerved him as well.

"But if you tell them there's a marijuana field and they bring in the DEA and maybe even the FBI..." She shivered as she imagined men in tactical gear with assault rifles charging into the midst of all those kids. This could turn into a horror show, and the blood would be on her and Russ's hands.

"Hey." He tugged her closer. "I'll be sure to mention the kids. Nobody wants anything to happen to them." He put a finger to her chin, tilted her face up to his, and smiled. Even in the midst of her agitation, his smile had the power to steal her breath. "First you think they're putting us in some kind of *Deliverance* scenario, and now you sound like you don't want me to report them. You can't think that they're right."

Right. That could be a tricky question, what was right. "No, they shouldn't be in the wilderness area, but I suppose their philosophy makes a kind of sense." Her mind began to fall into its familiar thought grooves, argument and counter-argument. "This land has been set aside for everyone to use, and they are using it. I mean, it is held in common by the government."

To a person of a certain persuasion, that argument would hold water. And Ash and Jilly were clearly that sort, which gave some insight into what they were doing here.

And gave her a hint of reassurance that she and Russ wouldn't be murdered tonight.

Russ raised an eyebrow. "Do you actually believe that, or are you playing devil's advocate?"

She got that a lot. "I'm only trying to understand their reasoning."

He made a quietly resigned noise. "Okay. Let me know when you're done so I can call."

"I'm done." She couldn't hide her amusement. And perhaps a hint of delight—it was a rare man who put up with her arguing and let her get on with it.

He released her, holding her at arm's length as he studied her face. "Sure you're okay?"

She took a deep breath. "Yeah. I'm—it'll be all right." It would. The fright remained—Ash still had that gun—but it was distant, more opaque now. She could handle what was left of the fear.

"Why don't you take a seat on the cot there"—Russ gestured to it—"I'll check that the coast is clear outside, then call the authorities. And then I can check your leg before we make our grand escape."

She took her first good look around the tent. There was an electric lamp, two cots with folded blankets, and a camp table with two stools. For a tent, it was practically homey. Although she supposed this *was* home for Ash and Jilly and the rest.

Holding very, very still, she listened hard for any noise outside the tent. Or even the vibrations of a presence there, not that she really believed in that stuff. But if her intuition suggested someone might be lurking, it wouldn't hurt to listen.

But there was nothing, no matter how she held her breath and strained to hear.

She took a seat on the edge of one of the cots. Jax came to lie at her feet, which really did make it homey. She pulled off her boots and then her socks, stretching her feet to work out some of the aches.

"Do I have to use Jilly's salve?" she asked. Rubbing something with Lord only knew what in it all over her leg didn't appeal.

"It's all-natural," he teased. "So it can't possibly hurt you."

"Hemlock is all-natural. So is radiation." The all-natural argument had never held water with her—she knew what nature was capable of.

"So's botulism toxin. And people still inject it into their faces."

She gave an exaggerated frown. "Not me. See all these wrinkles?"

He reached across and touched a finger to one. "I like them."

She swallowed, all of her crackling at that tiny touch. "Shouldn't you be calling the sheriff?"

He lifted his finger and she was suddenly cold, the crackles turning to goose bumps. She grabbed the edge of the cot tight, not wanting to grab her own arms and rub away that cold.

Russ rummaged in his pack before pulling out a portable phone charger. He motioned to her. "Give me your phone and I can charge it along with mine."

She handed it over. He plugged it in, then sat across from her, shorts straining across his thighs as he did, and pulled out his own phone. And immediately started cursing under his breath.

"What is it?" she asked.

"There's no signal."

Her stomach dropped. "What? What are we going to do now?" Suddenly bed murder seemed much, much likelier since they'd lost that avenue of escape.

He stared at the phone screen, glaring at it as if it had

gotten them into this mess. "I'm not sure. We could stay the night here, leave in the morning like they suggested, and call as soon as we can get a signal."

She didn't like that idea. Spending all that time among strangers, even if Russ and she weren't technically being held hostage, was a horrifying thought. And then an even worse one occurred to her: he'd told them they were married. She was going to have to pretend to be his wife if they did stay the night.

Her mouth fell open, and she felt as if the sourness flooding it might spill out. This was terrible. Utterly terrible. She couldn't even pretend to hold a normal conversation, much less be married to someone.

This time she did grab her arms.

"We could sneak away now," she said, her voice croaking a bit.

"We could." He sounded much less perturbed by all this than he should, although he kept whispering. "But then they'd know we're up to something. They might decide to come after us."

Oh God, being hunted through the wilderness by someone with a gun... In that case, she'd really rather stay here. Bed murder wasn't so bad next to that.

Not that either prospect was good.

She wrapped her arms more tightly around herself, the shivers threatening again. Jax set his head against her leg, all soft, fluffy, doggy comfort.

Lips pursed, she blew out all her fear and anxiety. Or at least as much of it as she could. "All right then. We stay here for the night and follow your plan." Her gaze caught on his. "And we'll have to pretend to be married."

His eyes went dark. "Yeah." The word seemed to scrape along her ears. "Do you have a problem with it?"

A problem. This was a little more than a *problem.* "No," she lied. "I'll be just fine."

"Right." That single syllable landed with a heated weight.

She curled her fingers around the cold metal tube of the cot frame, bracing herself against it. "Really." Her voice had a hairline crack. "I think I can handle this."

The fact that they had to whisper made the conversation that much more painfully intimate.

Professional. Professorial. She knew how to be those things, so why couldn't she be them right now?

"If you're sure."

He rose from the cot, and she leaned away before she could catch herself. Before she could reach out and grab him, pull his mouth down to hers.

A wife would lean close to her husband. Slowly she canted back toward him. "See? I can do this."

"Great. Take off your pants."

She gasped.

His smile was wickedly sweet. "So I can check your leg."

She glared at him as she hauled off her pants, determined to prove she wasn't embarrassed in the slightest. Although she really was. At least her cheeks felt cool—no blush to give her away.

He bent over her leg, the silk of his hair calling to her fingers. He had such thick hair, good for getting a nice fistful in the middle of a kiss. Or in the middle of other things.

Carefully he peeled away the gauze, studying the raw scrape beneath. "Looks good." His breath ghosted across her skin. "Want the salve?"

Salve? What— She blinked. "Do you think it needs it?"

"No." He took a fresh roll of gauze and began to rewrap her leg, his fingertips featherlight against her skin and electrifying all the same. "It doesn't look infected, although there is quite a bit of bruising."

"It feels better. Than before." Her voice wasn't working properly; that came out all wrong.

"Good." The word hit her bare skin like a caress. A quick glance from him. "Don't worry, I won't try to kiss you this time."

"Oh, that's too bad." She meant that to come out sarcastic, joking. Instead, it was a lament.

Oh, Bea. She didn't even have drunkenness as an excuse this time.

He pulled her to her feet, kept her hand tight in his. "You only have to ask."

She said nothing, just stared. Asking was so, so hard for her—didn't he understand that? He read her so well in everything else.

"Why don't you ask?" A dare from him.

And *why* didn't she just ask? What was wrong with her? All the reasons she shouldn't fluttered through her mind, but she couldn't catch them. She was much too preoccupied with him and his lips and his hands...

"Kiss me." Her mind finally caught something and it was *that*?

His lips quirked. "Not even a please?"

"No." She'd demand it. Asking was hard, but demanding was surprisingly easy.

The smile dropped from his face and he swooped.

This time, when she wasn't surprised or trying to fight her own need or inebriated... this time was transcendent. But she was still anchored, in him and herself and their bodies together.

She slipped her hands around his nipped waist, and his own hands found her ass and pulled her into him. He was already hard as hell, his erection an insistent thrust between them, and that made her melt. No man had ever been so excited so quickly by her. Being wanted so badly was a hell of an aphrodisiac.

His mouth was demanding, aggressive—there was nothing so weak as *likable* there. This was the Russ she'd slept with all those months ago, the one who'd haunted her erotic dreams.

He lifted her, straight up *lifted* her, then sat on the cot, pulling her astride him.

"How's your leg?" It was a growl.

"Fine." Oh, so breathy. That wasn't her, was it?

"Good." Then he was kissing her again and she was kissing him back. She didn't even feel the cold on her bare legs—it was too damn hot between them. He nudged her legs wider, his hips nestling deeper into hers. She wore only a pair of thin cotton panties, and she could feel the ridge of his fly against her sex—and the harder ridge of his cock.

He thrust up against her, almost experimentally. The fabric of his shorts caught her clit, and she gave a stuttering kind of moan.

"You like that, don't you?" When she didn't answer— couldn't answer—he said, "God forbid you actually admit it though."

He did it again, more assured this time. Her moan was just as fractured though.

"You like experiments, don't you?"

She didn't know why he was asking such a question when he was trying to shatter her brain, so she only nodded.

"We're going to try one here." He lifted his hips again, rubbed against her clit, and pleasure snapped through her. "Can you guess what my hypothesis is?"

She fought for enough breath to say, "My hypothesis is that you're a tease."

"Oh, I'll give you what you want. Eventually."

"You're always assuming you know what I want. What if you don't?"

He rubbed against her again. "I'd say your needs are pretty easy to read right now."

Smug bastard. She rolled her hips in a circle against his erection. "So are yours."

The demanding edge to his teasing slid away, leaving something more naked behind. "Not only in this moment. Since the first moment I saw you."

Words that were meant to please her but made her heart feel bruised instead. So she sidestepped. "You never said what your hypothesis was."

The edge returned to his dark gaze. "That I could make you come without taking any more of your clothes off. Or mine."

Oh, that would be a wonderful thing to test. But— "That's a damn shame, since I know how good you look with your clothes off."

"That's the first time this whole trip you've flirted with me."

She didn't want to think about that. "Less talking. More experimenting."

Flirting wasn't something that came easy, but experimenting... that she knew.

His grip tightened on her hips, sensation cascading through her from those two points. "Tell me if your leg hurts."

Legs? She had legs? All she could sense was the building need in her core, the insistent thrum in her clit that was demanding his touch. "Okay."

This time she met his thrust, determined to wring more sensation, more gratification, from that sweet friction between them. It was good, but not... She fisted her hands into his shirt, wanting to tear it off, to sink her nails into the skin and muscle she knew was under there.

He lifted his hips again, caught her clit again, and sparks stuttered through her. But it still wasn't enough. She released a moan of frustration.

"Hang on." He cupped her sex, her panties preventing the touch of his bare palm.

She shifted, trying to catch even a glancing brush of those fingers against her bare thigh. That was what she needed...

"Hang on," he repeated and began to draw circles on her clit. Or maybe the symbol for infinity. Or maybe... Oh, who cared what it was? She pressed against him, seeking more, and now.

But it didn't come.

Bea hissed out her exasperation. This wasn't going to work. She ought to just tear both their clothes off.

Then his fingers found a rhythm he hadn't yet explored. The frustration altered, transformed into a whetstone along the edge of her pleasure, each stroke making her need keener, sharper, until it was gleaming and dangerous—

She came in sharp, high climax, one that had her every muscle tightening to the breaking point as she tried to hold on through it. She had to grit her teeth hard to keep all the noises she wanted to make quiet in her throat.

"Goddamn, but that was amazing," he said, his eyes wide with wonder.

She could almost believe that he meant it, that seeing her get off was as good as getting off himself. But she knew that couldn't be true.

"It's your turn." She didn't bother to go slow as she unbuttoned his shorts and freed his cock—she knew he'd been ready for a while. The foreplay was done.

His cock was as she remembered—long and thick, it fit with his superhero persona. She stroked him from root to tip, then held him for a moment, warm and heavy in her hand as she savored the cooling dampness between her own legs. She was languid, satiated—and he was expectant, hungry. A gorgeous contrast.

"Hang on," she said and began to fist his length. A twist and a swirl around the head, down, down, down the silken length to where his cock met his body, dense hair meeting her hand. Her fingers fluttered out, brushed the heavy sac beneath, and then began their journey up again.

His breathing went rough, his gaze lidded as it centered on her. Her own breathing became labored, her nipples coming to hard attention since he looked as if he might eat her up. She increased her pace, found the bead at the tip and rubbed it into the head, watching him all the while as he watched her.

A slight hitch in his breathing, a jump of his hips as her hand cupped the head of his cock, and she knew he was close. She whipped his shirt off, taking the opportunity to test that magnificent chest of his with her nails.

At that scrape along his flesh, he came hard into his shirt, the muscles in his stomach tightening as he did. She could only watch in fascination as his entire body responded to his orgasm, muscles dancing, skin rippling, his eyes closing fully.

When he opened them again, he was smiling. Not with triumph, but fondly.

Uh-oh.

He cupped her face with his hand. "That was amazing too."

This was—was this part of his need to be liked? Was it only their forced proximity? Or something more? Something that couldn't be shaken when the adrenaline wore off?

This experiment of his was totally out of her control, and she hated that.

She needed distance, needed some space to think. So she took it. "Your hypothesis failed. You got naked."

His smiled dimmed. "Bea, don't do this." A warning.

"Do what?" She climbed off him, searching for her pants. As she pulled them on, she said, "You might want to put on a shirt."

"And here we go again. You know what? I don't think it's that you're reserved, or that you aren't friendly... I think you're scared. Scared that someone might discover that you have a softness under all that armor of yours."

His voice rose above a whisper. Not a shout, but still dangerously loud.

Again with the analysis! She wanted him to stop that, to stop testing for an exposed nerve. "You don't know the first thing about me. Don't play this off as if I have some kind of problem. I have friends. I've had boyfriends. I get along wonderfully with my family." She loved and was loved. She knew that. "You just can't stand that I'm not infatuated with you."

He stood, his bare chest inches from hers. "What I can't stand is that every time I get close to you, you freak out. Or you blame it on alcohol. But this time you can't. You weren't drunk and you weren't pretending. This was real... and it terrifies you."

"It should terrify you too!" She pulled her own voice back to a whisper, although it was utterly ridiculous to fight like this, hissing at each other like puff adders. "We're basically hostages here, and you want to make out and psychoanalyze me."

He shook his head. "You'll use any excuse not to see what's right in front of you, won't you?" He pulled a shirt from his pack and tugged it on. "I'm going out. Make sure Jax is settled when you leave."

He left her there, openmouthed and flabbergasted. And pissed that she hadn't gotten the last word.

Chapter 6

OF COURSE HE WOULD BE playing Hacky Sack.

Bea hung back by the tent and watched as Russ kicked around the little fabric bag with a circle of kids, their youthful faces turned toward him in a kind of worshipful reverence. These kids probably didn't see many new people —but there was something more. As if they were meeting a superhero. Or a fireman.

Somehow Russ has attracted these kids' adoration even without them knowing he was a firefighter. No doubt kids followed him through the grocery store with those exact same looks, wonderment and awe at seeing a superhero in the flesh.

He was a natural with them. He looked interested, and not just in one of them, but all of them.

And he was good at Hacky Sack.

She couldn't do what he did—simply insert herself into a situation and feel at home. Or fake it, if that's what he was doing. The unease was too great. And she so often had no idea what to say.

This right here, with him comfortably among strangers

and her hanging back quietly, was what it would be like to be in a relationship with him. He'd be in the middle of things, making friends, having fun—and she'd be on the outside, watching. Feeling out of place.

"So you're our guests for the evening."

She turned to find an older man coming toward her, moving as if his limbs pained him. He was breathing heavily too, as if his lungs were fighting him. He was about her height, maybe in his late fifties, with a shock of white hair that hadn't seen scissors in a while. But he had the hairline of a younger man, which she had the feeling he was rather vain about.

This must be Jilly's father.

"Hi. Yes. I'm... Bea." She couldn't remember if Russ had given them false names. She didn't think he had, but she'd been too keyed up to make a properly clear memory. If he had, she'd just given the entire game away.

"I'm Jake." He held out a hand, which she shook. "I heard you're injured."

Thank God she'd given the correct name. "Only a scrape. It's better now."

"Jilly's salve works wonders." Paternal pride infused the words. "I use it for the swelling in my legs."

Bea glanced at his legs, which were puffy, the skin stretched tight across them. "Oh." Judging by his labored breathing and his legs, the man had some kind of chronic condition. Maybe emphysema? Bea couldn't quite tell—she wasn't that kind of doctor. "You have a lovely... camp here."

That was the next stage of conversation: compliment someone on their home.

"Well, thank you. The girls have done so much work on it."

Bea wouldn't have called those two girls, especially not

Ash, but things probably looked different from Jake's vantage. "The kids seem very happy." And they did. Even with the ill-fitting clothes, they looked well cared for.

"We moved here for them, you know. To get them away from modern society and how it was poisoning them." The friendliness in his tone went dark as he said that last part.

"Oh." She knew they were crunchy, that they probably were off grid in more ways than one, but she had the feeling this conversation was about to go to a place that was the exact opposite of her own beliefs. "How interesting."

Jake didn't seem to hear her reluctance, because he gathered steam. "Yep. Had to get away from all that. I didn't use to believe it, but Jilly convinced me." His breathing went dangerously strained, his mouth working like a fish's as he pulled for air.

"Are you all right?" Her heart jumped into her throat—if he did need help, she wasn't certain what to do.

"Yeah." He gave a great guttering cough, which seemed to help. "I used to smoke. But being out here, it's saved me. And those kids."

He didn't sound saved. And it sounded worse than simply a smoker's cough. Perhaps it *was* emphysema. Not that it was any of her business.

"Well, good for you guys."

If he heard the fake enthusiasm in her voice, Jake didn't let on, or didn't care, because he started off on everything that was wrong with everything. He particularly got worked up about chemtrails and all the cancer they were causing— apparently cancer didn't exist before chemtrails—and the government's cover-up of the entire thing.

She wanted to scream, *That's not how it works! That's not how any of this works!* Instead, she murmured, "Hmm," although she didn't agree one bit. She even threw in a "How interesting," although she didn't find it interesting in the slightest.

"And that's why we stay in the wilderness areas." He was short of breath, but he didn't let that stop him. "To avoid the chemtrails. For the kids. It's too late for me, but we might be able to save them from the exposure."

In spite of herself, her heart twisted. She didn't agree with his notions, not at all, but she understood wanting to protect children. Of wanting the best future for them, even though she didn't have any of her own yet.

She looked at Russ, who was still playing with the kids. He would make a great dad. Easy, confident—he'd be self-assured with the kids and reassuring.

Bea would be more rigid in her parenting. She'd need someone softer to make up for it. She already knew that. Russ would do that nicely.

Funny what thoughts her brain sent forth out of nowhere. She and Russ certainly weren't ever having kids. After this camping trip from hell, they'd probably never see each other again, despite their recent mutual orgasms. There were some limits to biology.

"You guys don't have any kids?"

"Huh? Oh no. I'm uh... Well no, not yet. We're not quite ready." Not that it was anyone's business. Even if she and Russ were only pretending to be married.

"There's never a right time."

Oh, Bea had heard that one about a million times. No doubt every childless woman in America had at some point. If she confessed that she and Russ were only pretending— oh and by the way, Russ was also a firefighter about to call the authorities on them—would Jake say the same?

"Maybe," she hedged. "But this isn't the right time for us." Not that there ever would be a right time for them.

A thought occurred to her—out here in the wilderness, these children weren't going to school. They might not be getting any education at all. A creeping horror slid across her skin at the thought. "So..." She tried to be as a casual as she could so as not to reveal her true feelings. "Do you homeschool the kids?"

It was a ridiculous question on the face of it—what else would they do but homeschool, but she had to know what kind of education the kids were getting.

"Oh, we unschool."

She clenched her jaw to keep from groaning.

"They're interested in everything, these kids, so I do writing and reading with them, Ash does math, and Jilly does science. They really are amazing—even Nate, the littlest one, is already writing his own poetry."

"Really?" She studied Nate, who looked about six. That was impressive.

Russ caught her eye then, his smile slipping. Maybe he was still angry with her. Which was one of the more depressing thoughts she'd had recently. He clapped the kid next to him on the shoulder, said something that made the kid smile, then jogged over to them. His biceps made the most delightful bulges when he pumped his arms like that.

"Hey." He held out his hand. "I'm Russ. You must be Jake." He made it sound as if meeting Jake was the best thing that had happened to him today.

"Yep. Pleased to meet you." And Jake sounded as if he really meant it.

Bea waited for them to begin talking to each other, to slowly but inevitably push her outside the conversation.

Instead, Russ put an arm around her shoulders, drawing her close to put a kiss on her forehead. "How you feeling, babe?"

Wow. He was good. She knew he was acting and yet... she was convinced. "Um, okay." She wasn't half as good as he was though.

Jake didn't seem to notice. "Told you, Jilly's salve works wonders."

"It certainly did." Again, Russ sounded utterly convincing. But she knew he was lying.

What about all the other times he'd said that he liked her, that he wanted her to call, that he wanted another date with her? He'd sounded just as sincere then—but she had no idea if he was lying. And he'd proven he was very good at it, so good that it was hard to tell even when she knew for certain he was.

Even so, she nestled deeper under his arm. It felt good to be close to him. He was her only true ally here. And he smelled really, really good. Which he shouldn't have, being without a shower as long as he had.

She took a test sniff, searching for anything unpleasant in his scent. Nothing. How did he do that? It must have been one of his superpowers.

Jake was watching the kids with a fond smile. "Like I said, no good time. But the sooner the better."

"Pardon?"

Bea's face went hot at Russ's question. Because she knew that Jake was going to bring up kids.

"I was telling your wife that there's no good time to have kids."

She held her breath as she waited for Russ to answer that.

"We'll have kids when we're ready," he said mildly. "Or when Bea is ready—it's really her decision, not mine. And I'm happy when she's happy."

It was perhaps a perfect answer. Perfect enough to make

her throat burn. He pulled her closer, as if he knew how his words had affected her.

"Well, I'm just saying don't wait too long," Jake said.

No, Russ shouldn't wait too long to find someone to have kids with. He'd be great with them.

"Do they need help with dinner?" Russ asked.

Just like that, he steered the conversation away from the uncomfortable. Bea didn't even have to do anything—simply sit under his arm and let him do all the talking. It was a relief, really. She didn't have to think of what to say next, how to answer properly—and she wasn't on the outside, not with Russ holding her so close.

"Jilly and Ash have everything under control. In fact..." Jake cupped his hand around his mouth and yelled to the kids: "Time to get ready for supper!"

The kids dispersed quickly and without any grumbling. Bea had to admit they were very well behaved.

Jake waved good-bye as he followed them. "We'll all get ready. You folks enjoy the sunset."

Which left them alone. Russ kept his arm around her and they stared at the sun as it dipped below the horizon.

"Jax was okay when you left him?" His tone was neutral, neither inviting nor rejecting.

"Yeah. I gave him some water and food. He looked sad though." Poor Jax. It had almost broken her heart to leave him there.

A beat of silence. Then he said, "I'm sorry I yelled at you."

Her nose began to burn. She sniffed to clear away the sensation. "It's okay. This is a very stressful situation for both of us." It was perfectly natural that they would react so... wildly in such uncertain circumstances.

"It's not the stress of the situation that makes me want to kiss you. Among other things."

She wasn't certain she believed him. "We'll have to pretend to be a happy couple here." Best to focus on the here and now. Leave the past behind them. Even the past of thirty minutes ago.

"Think you can manage?"

She didn't, actually. It was a perfect storm of social anxiety and being attracted to him—oh, and the quasi-hostage situation. But there was no choice—she had to pretend she was in love with him. Or once had been, at least enough to marry him. "Yep. Should we go see about dinner?"

"No, let's wait until they call us. We can keep practicing at being married."

That answered the question of if he was holding her because he wanted to: it was only practice. Suddenly the weight of his arm was less a comfort and more a burden.

"Did you happen to check your phone recently?" he asked.

She nodded. "Right when I left our tent. Still nothing."

"If anything goes funky at dinner, you do exactly as I say, okay?"

"You don't really think something will happen, do you?" That's what he'd said before, but now it sounded as if he expected something to go down. "I mean, we're behaving as they'd expect from our story."

"I don't think they suspect anything, if that's what you mean, but if they do decide our story has too many holes— or if they find out we know about that field—things could get hairy fast."

Bea had no doubt Ash knew how to use that shotgun.

Best not to give her a reason. "Should we come up with a story?"

"One that can cover five years of being married? There's no way we could think up enough stuff."

"I was thinking that we'd only been married three years."

"Oh? Why not five?"

"I was doing my postdoc on the East Coast five years ago. How would we have met?"

He shook his head. "You never did a postdoc, remember? We're other people now."

That was right; she wasn't a scientist here. Which felt odd.

"I saw you when you were out visiting family and I was visiting Luke," Russ went on. "It was love at first sight—for me at least. You took more convincing."

That did make sense. "What kind of convincing?"

"I sent you handwritten letters professing my adoration."

"Really?" He didn't strike her as a letter-sending kind of guy.

He nodded. "Yep. After a few of those, you called me. Then I flew out to visit... and the rest is history."

"What did we do when you came out to visit me?"

He raised an eyebrow. "What do you think we did?" He smiled widely. "Went to hot pot of course."

"I can almost believe it." A wistful curve took hold of her lips because she really almost could. "It's a bit wasteful though, to send letters? With e-mail and all?"

"Not if it wins you the love of a good woman."

There was too much intensity in that for her to be comfortable. "I thought I was the one who quoted country songs."

Someone began to madly bang on a triangle.

"That's the dinner bell," Russ said. "Shall we go? Babe?"

She nodded, and he steered the both of them toward the next stage their deception would play out on.

SUPPER WASN'T HALF BAD. No meat, although Russ had been expecting that—it would be hard to keep meat out here, and they struck him as being vegetarians anyway. It was some kind of lentil and veggie dish, seasoned with harissa and served with flatbread. He took seconds, not only to be polite but also because he was ravenous.

The kids chatted about what they'd seen and done that day, encouraged by the adults. Even the unapproachable Ash unwound as the kids went on as kids did.

Speaking of unapproachable—he snuck a glance at Bea, sitting on his right. Her cool gray gaze was taking everything in, giving nothing back, exactly how she'd looked at him when he was playing Hacky Sack with the kids, as if they hadn't just gotten each other off and then argued about it.

He'd used the excuse of practicing being married to put his arm around her, to feel her close to him once more. Even now, his arm itched to set itself across her shoulders as he chatted with everyone. Something about having her nestled next to him made him feel... anchored.

Which he needed, since the more he got to know these people the worse he felt about having to turn them in. He wanted to unburden himself to Bea, to tell her all the reasons why he shouldn't call the authorities, because she would argue the opposite and remind him why he had to.

"So how did you two meet?" That was from Jilly.

Russ tossed Bea an indulgent smile. "Do you mind if I tell it? It's one of my favorite stories."

A flare of scorn flashed briefly in her eyes. The harder he played the role of besotted husband, the farther he pushed her away. In keeping her safe with this charade, he was probably destroying any chance he had of actually connecting with her.

"Of course." Her answering smile was strained.

He turned back to the group and slipped into his story-telling mode—canted forward, eyes bright, shoulders loose. Inviting them to come close and listen. "It all begins three years ago."

He caught Bea's half smile from the corner of his eye.

"A good friend of mine called me up and invited me to a barbeque at his family's place—Luke's his name. I said yes since I always had a good time with him. Little did I know that this would be more than a barbeque—that my entire life would change."

The expression on Bea's face was a mix of skepticism and curiosity, her full lips parted as the tip of her tongue came sliding along the seam there. She disliked that the story was made up... but she wanted to hear more.

"I decided to take Jax with me, and that was what saved me, as you'll see. I arrived, mingled and chatted with Luke's family, played some beanbag toss—just a usual Sunday barbeque, like a dozen others I'd been to."

He stopped, let the moment hang to get everyone to lean toward him. "And then Luke said to me, 'Hey, have you met my cousin? She's visiting from back east.'"

His gaze found hers, her expression now entirely rapt. "Luke led me over and she turned to me and I swear, it was like... like I can't even describe. I *knew* her, without even knowing her. And not a knowing that came from my brain, but from my very bones."

He flicked a glance at his listeners, wondering if he'd

gone too purple there. But they were openmouthed, wide-eyed, eager for the rest.

"In that moment I knew she was the one." He snapped his fingers. "Just that quick." A rueful smile and another pause to prepare his audience for the next. "But did she know it?" He shook his head.

Everyone laughed. Everyone except Bea, who had gone to solemn sadness.

"She wasn't impressed with me. Not even a little. Not matter what I said, she wouldn't budge." He stared at her hands, clasped in her lap, the knuckles white. "But Jax saved my bacon."

"How did he do that?"

At that question from Jilly, Russ realized he'd been staring at Bea's hands rather than telling the story.

"Ah well, she didn't fall in love with me at first sight… but she did fall in love with Jax. Sometimes I think that might be the only reason she stays with me—because of that dog."

Bea cleared her throat, the first noise she'd made the entire time. "He *is* a pretty awesome dog."

She was trying for humor, but the distance between her target and what she actually hit made his heart ache. Because she knew how long that distance was—he could tell from her face.

"That's not true." That was from Jake. "It's pretty clear you two are in love."

Judging by that comment and Jake's labored breathing, the man wasn't getting enough oxygen to his brain. Because Bea's discomfort with Russ couldn't be more clear. How could they not see it?

"Why didn't you like him right away?" asked one of the kids—Kellan was his name.

She took a moment to ponder before she said, "I… I misunderstood at first. I didn't think his feelings were real. They couldn't be, not that quickly and not under those circumstances. I don't believe easily." A quick sidelong glance from her. "I need to be convinced, and I'm hard to convince. Almost impossible."

"But Russ convinced you in the end?" Kellan said.

"Yes," she said slowly. "He did. Not right then, but eventually. Like I said, it took time. And different circumstances."

Russ's heart was working like a steam engine, all heat and pressure and pumping energy. If she was saying what he thought she was… then there was a chance for them. Outside these circumstances. In something more normal.

He could do normal with this woman. He suspected he could do normal for the rest of his life with her.

"Or you fell in love with his dog and decided taking the man along with it wasn't so bad," Jake teased.

She blushed. "Maybe. I definitely couldn't have one without the other."

Russ took the opportunity to put his arm around her. "I took *you* even without a dog."

"Yes, but I have my cats. And you love those cats."

He would love her cats, once he met them. "How could I forget the cats?"

"Wait." That from Ash. "You said she was visiting from the East Coast. What were you doing there?" she asked Bea.

"Working." A slight pause, in which she was probably trying to think of a suitable job. "I'm… an accountant."

An accountant and an engineer. Couldn't get more innocuous than that.

"Then you moved back here and then you got married," Kellan said decisively.

"What was the wedding like?" That from one of the girls

—Daisy. She didn't sound longing—more like intensely curious. As if they might describe their utterly alien rituals to her.

"We had it on my family's ranch," Bea put in. "That's where everyone in the family gets married."

Because there was a luxury resort on the family ranch, not that she was going to say so, Russ noted.

"Bea looked so, so beautiful," he told Daisy.

"Really?" Bea put in. "Because I'd been up all night, wondering if I was doing the right thing." Her gaze was pointed. "Wondering if you really wanted to spend the rest of your life with me and my idiosyncrasies."

He met her gaze measure for measure. "I didn't notice."

She was getting into the story now, warming up to the lie they were spinning between them, a little smile playing on her lips. "Blinded by love, hmm?"

"Yep. I can't see straight when I'm with you."

"You should see a doctor about that."

He almost, almost made a joke about how she was a doctor and did she want to take a look, but he caught himself just in time. "Unfortunately, I think the condition is chronic."

"Yep," Jake said. "You two are clearly crazy about each other."

"Yep," Russ agreed, still holding Bea's gaze. "Totally crazy."

For once she didn't contradict him.

Chapter 7

THE EASE OF THEIR PRETENSE was freaking Bea out.

They'd made up an entire story of how they'd met, with Russ looking deep into her eyes and telling her he was crazy about her... and she was buying it. No, more than that—she was *selling* it.

She could grow to like this sensation, of people staring at her with approval, hanging off her every word. Or rather, Russ's every word. She was the sidekick here, but she liked it. He took away the pressure of being witty and charming and thinking of things to say, and all she had to do was throw in something every so often. She could do that.

So she did it now. "Totally crazy, huh? And blinded by love? You might be past a doctor's help."

He leaned close and whispered in her ear. "I can think of one doctor who can help me."

She whispered back, "I'm not that kind of doctor."

"All right, you two," Ash said. Either she wasn't totally buying their story, or she found their lovey-dovey act offensive. Bea couldn't quite tell which.

"Sorry," Russ said with his hundred-watt smile. "I know

111

we're supposed to be past the honeymoon stage, but I can't help it."

They'd never even had a honeymoon stage. "You're making everyone sick," Bea said, tartness creeping back into her tone. It was fun, yes, to banter with him like this, but they were also lying here. She'd do well to remember that.

There was a moment of silence signaling the end of their interlude, and then Jilly clapped her hands for everyone's attention. "Everyone done? Let's clean up then."

Russ snapped to his feet. "Can we help?"

Such a Boy Scout.

"No, you two relax," Jilly said. "You're our guests."

Ash flicked a look at them. She had invited them but clearly didn't want them to overstay their welcome.

The kids cleaned up along with Jilly. Jake and Ash stayed seated along with Bea and Russ, making it clear where those two were in the hierarchy here. Jake was probably exempt thanks to his illness. And Ash was the leader—there was no longer any doubt of that.

Bea's discomfort grew as they cleared up around her. She didn't need to be waited on, and the way Ash was staring at her was almost challenging. Bea didn't get what her problem was—the woman had practically insisted that they stay.

Once that was done, Ash announced, "Let's go outside."

Someone—maybe one of the kids—had set up a propane heater in the middle of a ring of chairs. The night had a biting chill, and Bea shivered as she walked to the ring.

"I'll get you a jacket and a hat," Russ said low and only to her. "They're in your pack, right?" He took her elbow and leaned over her as he spoke, the heat from his body radiating onto her.

"Um, yes."

When he left, her sense of safety, of belonging to someone other than herself, vanished. She would have to keep up the pretense all on her own, which made her feel completely alone.

"You can't see even half these stars in so-called civilization," Jake said as she took the chair next to him. His breathing had grown worse, his expression strained—as if something were choking him.

"Are you all right?" she asked.

He gave a short shake of his head. "Just get a little winded after I walk sometimes. It'll stop soon."

She watched him carefully, wondering if she needed to call for Russ. Of course, once Russ demonstrated his super paramedic skills for everyone, the jig would be up.

"Look at the stars," Jake urged.

She craned her neck, taking in the glittering field sprouting from the black soil of the night. She'd seen the stars like this before, on her other hiking trips, but she had the sense Jake was trying to share something special with her. So she said, "That's amazing." And really it was, no matter how many times she'd seen it.

Jake gestured with his forefinger, tracing out a pearly swirl stretching across the sky. "Most people never even see the Milky Way anymore—isn't that sad?"

"It is." She might not agree with him about chemtrails and alternative medicine and using federal reserves as camping grounds, but she could agree with that.

"Here comes your man."

She turned to see Russ coming toward her, wrapped in a jacket, hat pulled over his ears, and carrying her stuff.

Her man. The charade between them was already

fogging her brain, making her want to believe that was true, that he really was her man.

She stood, reached out her hands for her stuff, but Russ gestured for her to turn around. When she did, he helped her into her jacket, even zipping it up for her. He tugged the hat onto her head, messing up her hair when he did, and even slipped her gloves onto her hands. Bea hadn't been so passively dressed since she was maybe five—being the independent sort, she'd started demanding to dress herself at an early age, even with the tricky stuff she couldn't always manage on her own.

While Russ was outfitting her, Jilly and Ash came to sit by the heater. When Russ went to find a seat, there weren't any.

Bea gestured to hers. "You can take mine. Or..." She looked around but could only see the benches along the picnic tables. Maybe she could go back and get one of the stools from the tent. That would be uncomfortable after a while though...

"No worries." Russ picked her up—as if he did it all the time—and set himself in her chair and her in his lap. "This'll work."

The impulse to be embarrassed or anxious didn't come, not even in the slightest. Probably because it would have given them away and she was growing into their charade. She set her cheek against his chest and his arms came around her. There. No one would think they were anything but a loving married couple.

Ash was filling tin cups from a bottle and passing them around. "I guess you two will want to share."

It was flat rather than sharp. Maybe Ash didn't resent them. Or maybe that's just how she was—reserved. Bea could sympathize.

Russ took the cup from her. "Thanks. We will." He sniffed it and then took a sip. "It's tequila," he said in a low tone to her. "Do you want some?"

There was more under the words—another question beyond that. No doubt related to her behavior on their one date.

But he didn't know that she actually liked tequila—good tequila, made with pure agave and aged properly, not the stuff that one usually found slopped into a margarita. Not that she didn't like margaritas—there was a time for those as well.

She took the cup and sniffed it herself. Huh. This might actually be decent tequila. She took a sip and raised her brows. Wow. It was.

"What is this?" she asked.

"Tequila," Jilly said. "But from Mexico. That's where we like to spend the winters."

That explained it. "It's good."

Russ put his mouth to her ear. "I never would have guessed."

There was a lot about her he didn't know. An entire life beyond this crazed hiking trip.

"Man, you guys can't stop with the sweet nothings, can you?" Jilly was trying to be joking, but there was something off in her tone.

Russ raised his head but kept rubbing a hand along Bea's arm. "Like I said, we never really left the honeymoon stage." He took another sip. "This is really good. Where do you guys stay in Mexico?"

The others went still and quiet. "Here and there," was all Ash said.

Hmm. Even Russ could put a foot wrong it seemed. She took the cup from him and took another fortifying sip, warmth beginning to pulse through her. Time to change the subject.

"How many shooting stars do you think we'll see tonight?"

"Oh, at least one or two," Jake said. "One night we must have seen two dozen, just one right after the other in about five minutes. A shower of them. That was gorgeous."

Russ set his chin on her head. "I wish we could have seen it. Don't you?"

He smelled not like soap, but warmer, more comforting than that. And a hint of something primal beneath.

"Yeah," she said. Her bones seemed to be languidly liquefying, perhaps due to the tequila. Or due to cuddling so close to him. Or probably both—Russ plus alcohol multiplied by herself equaled stupid levels of sexual attraction.

She took another sip of the tequila. It'd be a shame to waste any of it, but once she reached the end of this cup, that was it. She'd learned her lesson the last time.

Russ began chatting with Jake about shooting stars and which constellations were which. She was impressed he knew so many—she liked picking out actual stars rather than shapes that didn't really look like anything. Like Betelgeuse or Sirius or...

She woke what felt like half a second later. Only the chairs around them were empty and Russ was still holding her as the heater glowed red.

His arms tightened around her as she jerked awake. She rubbed her eyes and scrubbed some of the drool from her lips. *So attractive.* "Sorry," she mumbled.

"It's okay." His voice was as dark and deep as the night surrounding them.

"When did they all leave?"

"I'm not exactly sure. A while ago."

She dropped her voice even lower than his. "Do you think they know? About us? About the field?"

"No. Ash made it clear tonight—she expects us to leave tomorrow morning."

"Do you think she suspects?" Out of all of them, Bea was most worried about Ash. She knew that narrowed-eyed skepticism—it fueled so many of her own investigations.

"No. I think that's just how she is."

He was pretty good at reading people, so he was probably right. Silence spread between them as they both looked out at the night.

"How's your leg?"

"It's much better. Resting it today helped."

"Good."

He made no move to rise or remove her from his lap. "Aren't you cold?"

"A little."

He must have been more than a little cold—she was close to frozen. But she didn't try to get up either.

"Why didn't you wake me?" she asked. He was strong, that was for sure, but his legs must be asleep by now.

"I was enjoying myself."

"Was?"

"Am."

Feeling daring, she slipped a hand around his neck, nestled her face into the crook of his neck and jaw.

"Bea?" He was back to growly again.

"Yes?" She buried her nose into his bare skin there, savoring his scent.

"Are you drunk?"

"No." She was warm, buzzing from the tequila—but she wasn't incapacitated.

"But you were drinking. Like last time. And you regretted it."

She couldn't deny that. "But you were drinking too tonight. This time we're balanced."

"You still might regret it in the morning."

She might. Right now it felt good and right, but it had felt that way the last time too. And in the cold light of morning, she'd realized what she'd done.

She breathed a kiss against his neck. "I might regret it in the morning. You might too. But for now it feels right."

His hand came heavy on the back of her neck. "Don't tease me, Bea. You can't run off tomorrow morning."

A shiver ran through her, a lightning strike of delicious fear. This was the Russell who meant to be obeyed, the one who'd taken charge when she'd hurt herself. He didn't know it, but his becoming that man made her want him more. To tell her again that he had her, that she couldn't run, that he'd hold tight and keep turning her toward him no matter how she averted her face.

Normal Bea, the Bea who lived in her office and was an ambitious scientist, would be horrified. But this Bea wanted it. Wanted it until the taste of her need spread copper sparks thick across her tongue. "Please," she begged, the word heavy with that need.

He made a resigned noise. "I don't know what to do with you."

"Yes you do. You've done it before."

That caught him nice and tight she could tell—his thighs went rigid beneath her and she could feel his cock insistent against her ass.

"Beatriz." A growly warning of a mating call. And the way he pronounced her name...

"Do you speak Spanish?"

"A little bit," he said. "Do you speak Mandarin?"

"No. Although I do speak Japanese."

"Where did you learn Japanese?"

"We had a private tutor. Our great-grandfather was Japanese—our branch of the family always has to learn at least some of it."

"You're part Japanese." He groaned. "Don't ever tell my mother that."

"When would I meet your mother?"

With that, it was ended. The tension left him, a loose resignation stealing through him. "That's right. You won't. This is just for tonight. Or however long *you* like."

Her anxiety and unease came crashing back and forced her half off his lap. "I'm sorry. I should have known that... that you wouldn't want this. I'm so, so sorry." Stupid Bea, trying to be some kind of seductress and looking like an idiot instead.

He caught her wrist, pulled her back down. "That's not what I meant." His breath was harsh in her ear. "You..." Another harsh inhale. Then: "Fuck it."

His mouth captured hers.

Chapter 8

BEA OPENED LIKE A FLOWER under his kiss. He was the sun and her petals unfurled toward him. Or something like that. Tequila made bad poetry flow through her.

His mouth was making heat flow through her, their tongues sliding together, the side of her breast rubbing against his chest. But she wanted more, wanted only naked heat between them. Her clit was already pulsing, begging for attention.

She fisted a hand in his jacket and tugged him even closer. "Let's go to the tent," she said against his mouth.

He rose in a smooth motion, clasping her to him. God, they must look like the cover of a romance novel, the hunky man carrying the dainty heroine like it was nothing. Or maybe a comic book, with the muscled superhero carrying his ladylove to safety.

Bea looked nothing like the women on those covers, but he made her feel like she could be one.

"You're pretty good at this," she said.

"Carrying you?"

"Yep. Do this often? Carrying women back to your bed?"

"Nope. Just you."

"Really?" she asked. "You'd never done that before? I was your first? Wow, I'd never have been able to tell."

He laughed. "Hardly. I *am* a fireman and you know how crazy we make the ladies." He went serious. "Bea, are you sure you're not drunk?"

"I swear, I'm not. It's just... you make me silly sometimes." A hard thing for her to confess, but his arms around her made it easier.

"I like that. That you want to be silly with me."

"Now's your opportunity to impart a big life lesson to me," she said, trying to inject some lightness, "to tell me that I should be silly more often, that I should enjoy life more."

"Nope. I don't agree with any of that." That was unexpected. "Well, maybe the enjoy life more part. But you should be doing that with me. And I want you to save all that silliness for me. Nobody else gets it."

"Rather possessive of you, isn't it?" That was also unexpected.

"I bet you have a little streak of jealousy too."

"Nope." She patted his chest. Damn, but it was solid. "I'm enlightened."

"Ah. So if I told you that I was half-naked in a charity calendar, you wouldn't care?"

"Not a bit." Although, half-naked was... He didn't really mean half-naked. Just his shirt open or something.

"Not even if you knew that hundreds of other women were ogling my picture?" he asked.

Well, that wasn't cool. But— "It's for charity. I can't begrudge anything so noble." Except she could, something sharp and cold twisting in her belly when she thought of all those strange eyes roaming over him.

"Oh, then all the fan mail I get won't bug you. And the pictures they send me—"

"Pictures?" She stiffened in his arms. "Good Lord. Pictures of what?"

"Oh…" He was all fake innocence. "Just poses and such. Things they think I might like. And the letters talk about how *inspiring* they find my picture."

Bea just bet they did. "What month were you?"

"July. Right in the center."

He was a centerfold. A centerfold firefighter who seemed to think she was amazing and was about to rock her world. Again. The world was a crazy place.

They'd reached the tent, and he lowered her to the ground. She swept into the tent before she lost her nerve about bedding Mr. July.

Jax greeted her with a wriggling butt and a lick of her hand. "Hey, dude." She rubbed his ears. "Did you miss us? I told you we'd come back."

Russ came in behind her. "Jax. Wait outside."

The dog went and lay outside the tent flap.

"Come here," he ordered her.

He was back to commanding Russ. Oh yes, this was what she'd wanted. "What are you going to do to me?" A little coy, a little breathless. A little bit of a game here.

"I told you to get over here." Simply stated and all the more lust-inducing for being so calm. He was going to ruin her, she could already tell.

She went to stand before him. "Right here?"

His fingers caught the tab of her jacket zipper and slowly dragged it down. "That'll do. For now." The zipper released with a soft pop. "Do you know how long I've wanted to do this?"

She shook her head.

"Since you came out of the car at the trailhead." He slipped the jacket from her shoulders. "No, since before then. I thought about you after our date. So often."

"Why didn't you call?"

He nipped at her lower lip. "I wanted you to come to me."

She caught her breath. And then gave him the entire secret of herself: "You can never rely on me to come to you. I never do."

He breathed a kiss at the corner of her mouth. "You came to me tonight."

She hadn't, not really. This was an odd, in-between state for them. She could leap to him when she was stretched out over the crevasse. On stable ground, things would be different.

But now was the earthquake, and she could be unsteady here. She threaded her hands into his thick hair, heavy and soft as silk, and pulled him to her for a scorching kiss. When she came up for air, she asked, "What are you going to do to me?"

"First, I'm going to finish undressing you." His fingers found the button of her jeans, flicked it open. "How's your leg?"

Ah, even when he was commanding, Russ was caring. "Don't worry about that." She certainly wasn't.

He slipped off her shirt, tossing it aside. His hands came back to frame her breasts, his thumbs finding her nipples through her bra. She breathed into the moment, at the touch she'd remembered and longed for so many times. He breathed with her, the two of them joined by more than touch in that moment. His hands slid around her back, released her bra—and then it was bare skin on bare skin.

She lifted toward him, her body yearning for his in the only way it knew how. Begging, in the only way it knew how.

Only, perhaps not the only way. Already there was damp heat building in her core, a pulsing urge that needed his bare skin against that as well.

His thumbs teased her nipples, and then he took them between his fingers and pressed. Hard enough to have her gasping. "Beautiful," he said, and she couldn't tell if he meant her breasts or her reaction. Or both.

He did it again, and heat flooded her pussy as it clenched around emptiness. And again and again until she was close to sobbing, her hips lifting with each press, begging him for relief.

He set a hand at her jaw, stared straight at her as she stared back bleary-eyed. "So beautiful," he repeated.

She wrapped her hand around his wrist. "I need you."

"You have me."

She unzipped his jacket with a sharp rip, tore it from his shoulders. Then off with his shirt and finally, finally she had his bare chest before her. She lightly ran her hands over him, over rippling abs and hard pecs and tight shoulders.

"Did you wear your uniform? In the calendar?"

"Um…" His chest worked as if his lungs weren't quite drawing enough air. "I wore my turnouts."

"Just the pants though, right?" She could see it, the yellow pants riding low on his hips, the divots of his hips in sharp relief.

"Yeah." She had the feeling he didn't even know what she'd asked.

"And your suspenders…" She ran her hands along where they would have been. "They would have lain right here. But you don't have any suspenders now." She flicked open his jeans, pushed them down and away. "So you shouldn't have any pants either."

As she rose from helping him out of them, she ran a quick hand over his straining cock, giving a squeeze. He groaned, then fisted his hand in her hair and devoured her mouth. She reached for him again, gripping him and savoring the moans she could draw from him. So good, those sounds were so good.

"Wait." He tore his mouth from hers but didn't pull her hand away from his cock. "You're still wearing pants." He had them off her quicker than she could have imagined before pushing her back toward the cot. "Sit down."

Her knees went weak at his tone and the cot caught her. He knelt at her feet, set his hands at her knees, and opened her thighs.

"Beautiful." He'd said that before, but this time the reverence went so deep as to steal her breath. Utterly. Completely. There was nothing left in her.

He lowered his mouth and she filled again with pleasure and heat and need. He wasn't gentle about it, not that she wanted gentleness. He devoured her pussy much as he had her mouth earlier, sucking and lapping and worshiping her with his tongue and lips. She put a hand to his head and lifted her hips, greedy in her need.

That greed only fed his hunger, low noises escaping his throat as he sucked on her clit. That was what sent her over the edge, that *noise* coming from him, eager and happy and wanting more.

She collapsed back on the cot, rubbery and boneless and so well pleasured she couldn't even form a proper thought.

But still there remained an... urge. A need. Deeper than the climax she'd just achieved could reach.

She propped herself on her elbows and looked at him. "Oh my God, do you even have any condoms?"

Not elegant, not sexy, but she couldn't help but blurt that out. He made her silly.

"Yep." His smile told her he was charmed. "The Boy Scout motto: always be prepared."

"Of course you were a Boy Scout. Of course." It went along with the whole Superman-American-Way thing he had going on.

"Nope." He grinned. "I never actually was. But it's a good motto."

"I'm not going to argue about that right now." She was too relieved to know that he'd be inside her soon, so soon. But first... She slipped off the edge of the cot, knelt between his thighs. The ground under the tent floor was uneven beneath her knees, but she welcomed the reminder of the unevenness of their situation. She looked up at him, gripping the base of his cock as she did. The look he sent her in return was intent, intense. Full of warm darkness.

She held his gaze as she took him deep into her mouth, as deeply as she could. The head nudged the back of her throat, making her eyes water. It was awkward and uncomfortable, but also intimate and open. She pulled back, swirled her tongue around the crown, and took him deep again. He tasted of salt and tang and a hint of sweetness. He began to make those noises again, the ones that had made her so crazy, little grunts of pleasure and greed. He ran his fingertips along her jaw, threaded them through her hair, and caressed her as she sucked him deep.

But then he was pulling away. "I need you."

"I want you."

He cupped her face, running a thumb across her cheekbone, all tender possessiveness. He kissed her the same way, making her heart do strange, painful things. Before she could tell him to stop, before her heart cracked, he was settling himself on the cot, pulling her astride him. His hand reached down, came back with a foil packet. They put the condom on together.

When it was done, he set his hands at her hips, held her above him. "Ready?"

She wasn't—and yet, they'd been building to this since that horrible, wonderful date. "Yes." *No. I don't know.*

But it was too late, because half a moment later he was deep within her and it was so, so good. That urge that had been building, the one that her previous climax couldn't reach... it began to ease, to resolve as he moved with her. She rolled her hips to meet his, catching his rhythm. His pubic bone caught on her clit as he made a pleased grunt, and she had to shut her eyes. Too much, but God she needed more.

His fingers sank tight into her hips, anchoring her as he drove even deeper. She clutched at his shoulders, needing some balance as the rhythm grew wilder, faster.

"Beatriz. Beatriz." He called to her to join him as he approached his orgasm, the harsh command he made of her name—simply her name—sending her rushing toward her climax. That and his fingers at her clit now, working in time with his cock, her name and his touch making a carnal melody on her body.

She came and came hard for the second time that night. A moment later he came as well, eyes closed, jaw tight, the pleasure wracking him as it spent.

She folded over him, feeling damp and sticky sweat on the both of them. They were going to be freezing in a few moments. Before she even finished the thought, she shivered.

He put his arm around her. "Hang on. I've got a blanket." As if by magic, he pulled one from under the cot and pulled it over her, keeping her lying across him. "Comfortable?"

Comfortable wasn't quite the word. The cot was narrow, her leg had begun to throb, and she realized she was dead tired—but she didn't want to be anywhere else. "Yep. You?"

"Yep. Got a nice blanket here. Warm."

"I hardly make a good blanket."

"No, you're the *best*."

"I'm not very fuzzy."

"You're fuzzy inside, which is what counts."

She wasn't though. She really wasn't. "Are you sure you can sleep like this? You can say if you want to have separate cots."

"If I wanted separate cots, I'd have said so." He was a little irritated, but mostly sleepy. "Do you?"

She could take the safe route here, finally. After all the unstable things she'd done tonight, here was her retreat. Come tomorrow, she could retreat even further. Until she was back in her safe, reserved shell, with him on the outside.

The safe route didn't appeal though. His big body, his heavy arm around her waist, the warm scent of him—that appealed.

"No," she said. "I can sleep here."

"Good. Are you warm enough?"

She nodded against his chest. She would be soon enough with his heat surrounding her.

"And your leg?"

It ached a bit, but nothing that she couldn't handle. "It's fine. I'm ready to press on tomorrow."

"Yeah. Tomorrow." Russ didn't sound eager to greet it.

Neither was she.

Chapter 9

SHE WAS IN HIS ARMS.

Morning had come, soft and still on chill gray feet. Bea's head was tucked under his chin and some of her hair had caught in the stubble on his jaw. Even after two days in the wilds, she smelled faintly of tea roses. It was a little old-fashioned, that scent, but it suited her. He could imagine her wearing a thin cardigan and black trousers in all her professorial glory, with the hint of tea roses clinging to her.

He really liked her.

Maybe she was right, that he just liked everyone by default and needed everyone to like him. He could admit it —he cared that people had a good time with him.

But with her, it was deeper. It *mattered* to him that she liked him.

Russ had watched her struggle to contain herself as Jake had talked about chemtrails and the government poisoning everyone. She'd thought it the worst nonsense she'd ever heard—and she'd still been polite, noncommittal. She was trained to root out nonsense and destroy it, so for her to do that... Russ knew what it meant for her to do that.

And this plant. She was doing all this for her lab. For all the people depending on her. For future patients she might never meet. He wondered if anyone in her lab would appreciate what she'd been through here. He had the feeling she'd never tell them what had happened.

She opened her eyes and blinked at him. "Hey." Solemn. A touch embarrassed.

There was no need for that. "Hey." He smiled widely at her.

She smiled back, relief easing across her face. "We survived."

"Yep." They had only to pack up and hike out of here. "Now we can finally go get your plant."

Her smile went rigid. "And you can report this nest of criminals."

That was a little too pointed for his liking. "They're not bad people. But... Well, this can't go on." Even Bea should be able to see that.

"And that offends your superhero sense of justice?" She clearly liked to harp on the superhero/firefighter thing with him.

"You can't even decide if it's right or wrong."

"I just like to consider both sides of a story." She pushed herself up and away from him. "Even after I've decided."

She sat on a fence and judged it all from afar, and he ran in and slobbered over everyone. Not a great analogy, but holding her close like this while they argued was making him irritable. Couldn't they just enjoy this?

"It doesn't seem like you considered both sides of the story with me," he said.

"I don't understand."

"Even though we had a great time on that date, you decided you'd never call. And even though we had a great time here—and I made you come three times yesterday, and don't tell me other dudes have done that for you on the regular—you're going to pull the same shit." He didn't bother to keep his tone anything like friendly or nice. He was pissed and he wanted her to know it.

"I beg your pardon." She stood, pulling the blanket around her. "I don't owe you anything."

"No. No, you don't." God, he sounded like he was begging her to like him, but he couldn't help it. "I just... I don't understand why you won't even consider dating me."

She rubbed a hand down her leg—the good one. "Because... because you want everyone to like you. I don't know if you want me to call so you can keep your perfect record of everyone being your friend or if you're really interested in me. As a person." She ducked her head. "I know I'm not an easy person to like. I'm okay with that. I'm not going to change to make you happy. I might be unlikable, but I like myself."

He still didn't understand. "I like you too."

"But how do you know?" She gestured between them. "We've only interacted under the most extreme circumstances—and yes, someone buying you as my date and drunken karaoke at hot pot counts as extreme—which could be clouding your judgment. We've never done anything normal together. How do you know that you won't hate how I brush my teeth?"

"We've survived the camping trip from hell together. The day-to-day should be easy after that. I mean, at least we can try."

She tucked the blanket tighter around her as she frowned at the floor. "I don't know."

Meaning: *No.* He could read her well enough to see that. "You claim to look at every side, but what good is that if you never change your mind?" He shook his head. "Forget it. You're right. I probably wouldn't be happy with someone so inflexible."

He could see that hurt her, her mouth turning down and her shoulders drooping. "I told you I was unlikable."

All right, now he was being an asshole. "Hey." He reached for her hand, but she sidled out of reach. "Sorry I said that. That was unkind."

"It's okay." But she kept out of his reach.

"Listen, I get that you don't want to date. I won't ask again." Sourness filled his mouth at the thought, but he'd keep to it. "But maybe we can be friends? At least for the rest of this trip? Then you won't have to see me again. No more reminders of that terrible date or this terrible trip, I promise."

She didn't look as happy about that as he'd expected. "Of course we can be friends. I appreciate everything you've done, and I'm sorry it's been so awful for you."

It hadn't been awful. He'd gotten to know her better, which had been awesome. But he was tired of trying to explain himself to her—they didn't seem to speak the same language. Or she was determined to misunderstand.

Whichever it was, he was done. "Should we pack up and head out?" Grudging, but he didn't feel like hitting friendly.

"Yeah."

Russ hefted his pack onto his back and snapped for Jax. The dog looked between him and Bea, uncertainty in his mismatched eyes.

Poor Jax. He was confused by their argument.

"Come on, Jax. You need to go out."

Jax slunk out after him. Crap. Even his dog was crazy about Bea. *She doesn't want us, dude. Just let it go.*

The camp was quiet in the dawn, the weak light turning

everything gray and pink and gold. The kids were quietly eating breakfast with no sign of any adults. Or wait—there was Jake, coming out of his own tent.

"Morning."

"Morning." Russ studied the man. He did not look well. His breathing was rattled, harsh. "How are you feeling?"

Jake waved that off. "It's always tough in the mornings."

It looked especially tough to Russ, but he kept his peace. He wasn't here to rescue anyone.

"Are Jilly and Ash around?" Russ asked. "I'd like to thank them."

"Jilly sleeps in most mornings, and Ash is off on some errands."

Checking the field, most likely. He and Bea would have to steer well clear of it on the hike out.

He held out a hand to Jake. "Well, thank you for having us. We enjoyed it."

"Of course. I hope your wife is feeling better."

Russ held tight to his smile. "She certainly is."

His wife came toward them then, her face set in grim lines, but her gait easy and smooth. No hitch of pain there.

"Ready, babe?" He still had to pretend, no matter how it stung.

"Yes." She'd already dropped the pretense of being enraptured by him. "Thank you very much for your hospitality," she said to Jake. "Please tell Jilly and Ash thank you for us when you see them." Grave, correct, and distant.

The real Bea had returned. Or at least the Bea she preferred to be.

"I'll do that," Jake said. "You folks take care."

"You too." There was an odd catch in her voice.

She was probably feeling guilty about what Russ would have to do once they had a cell signal. Hell, even

Russ felt guilty about it. But not guilty enough to give them away.

"Yep, enjoy Mexico this winter," he said as he reached for Bea's elbow. He thought about adding something about seeing a doctor if Jake started to feel worse but decided against it. Although the man really did look worse than yesterday. His color was off—

Bea pulled her elbow from his grip and started out of camp. "Good-bye," she called over her shoulder.

Russ touched his forehead in farewell. "See you."

The kids followed them for a while, yelling good-bye and asking when they'd see them again. Russ would only say he didn't know. Eventually the kids turned back for home, leaving just him and Bea and Jax.

And utter, total silence. They made their way back to the official trail, Bea setting a fierce pace.

When they finally stepped onto the main trail, she swung on him. "Well? Aren't you going to call the authorities?"

"Once we get your plants."

He took grim pleasure in the sight of her mouth dropping open.

"But I thought—"

"We're here for those blooms, aren't we? The ones that so many people are depending on. So let's get the damn things. I'll make the call once you're finished."

He hadn't planned to do that—he'd meant to call and then seek out the blooms if they still could. But something about her attitude today, the way she'd pushed him away yet again, made him want to set her off-balance. To give her a little push and watch her stumble.

Once this was over, she couldn't claim she hadn't gotten exactly what she'd wanted.

"You're upset," she said. Quiet and a touch hurt.

"Yeah. I get that way sometimes. I'm not all sunniness and begging for everyone's approval all the time."

He was being a dick, he knew he was being a dick—but he still wanted to get that out. To puncture her notions of him, especially the ones she meant to use as a shield between them.

Maybe he wasn't as done with her as he'd thought he was.

"I never said that," she said.

She hadn't. And he was a shit for bringing it up. "Fine. Do you want to get this plant or not? If not, I'll get out my phone."

"You might not have a signal yet."

Logic. Always with the logic from her. "That doesn't answer my question. What do you want to do?"

She set her jaw. "I want my plant. But you already knew that. And I'm sorry my need to preserve my career is ruining your chance to play the hero. But I would have thought you got enough of that at work."

Okay, now *she* was being a dick. "Let's go then. I'll lead."

He didn't wait to see if she followed. Jax trotted at his heels, whining every so often, which made Russ worry that she wasn't keeping up. But he wouldn't look since he could hear the crunch of her boots in the dirt. Jax was only upset because they were fighting. Again.

When they came within a mile of the pot field, Russ veered off the trail, taking them through heavy scrub that pulled and scratched at them.

She made no noise of complaint, didn't ask what he was doing. Just followed like a robot.

If she had asked, he would have said he was taking them to another trail that branched off from a point on the other side of the pot field, one that would get them close to her precious penstemon field. For a savage moment he wished that they would get there and find nothing. That they would both leave this trip utterly empty-handed.

He was being a dick again.

After about an hour of hard going through the uncut scrub brush, their phones began to beep and ding and make every other alert noise they were capable of.

They'd gotten a signal again.

Russ fished his phone out of his pocket and unlocked the screen.

Bea stared at him, half defiant, half inquiring. "Are you going to call the sheriff now?"

Her tone had his irritation rising again. "No. I told you I'd do it after. I want to meet them there, make sure they understand the situation. Can't do that if I'm taking you to your plants."

She flushed and looked away.

He looked down at his phone, anger and a touch of shame burning his own cheeks as he scrolled through the novel of texts his mother and sisters had sent him.

I'm fine, he sent out to all of them. *Lost the signal. Happens all the time, as you already know.*

But they panicked each and every time because they loved him.

There was a message from Luke too: *How's it going? Bringing my cousin back in one piece?*

That was going to be a very interesting conversation when Russ tried to explain everything to Luke. Not that he probably could, not if he couldn't mention their one-night stand.

Yep. Going to take an extra day though.

Luke must have been right by the phone, because just next came: *Heard about the trouble from Lil. Everything okay?*

No, and why did you send me on this trip with your cousin who I kind of might adore but wants nothing to do with me?

Russ didn't send that—it wasn't Luke's fault.

He deleted it and typed, *Everything's fine.*

A message torn out from Bea's playbook, but it worked. There were no more texts from Luke.

Russ locked the phone and slid it back into his pocket. He heard Bea speaking into hers from behind him, her whispers urgent. And then quiet.

No, not quiet. There was some sniffling there—very small, muffled sniffling, the kind the person doing the sniffling most definitely did not want anyone to notice.

Bea was crying.

He wanted to turn, to gather her up in his arms, to call over Jax to cuddle close to her. He wanted to make it all better.

Don't be a hero, Cheng. She doesn't want your help.

"Are you ready?" he asked. He did give her the courtesy of not looking at her though.

A watery inhale, and a sound that was perhaps her wiping her eyes. "Yes."

Fuck, he just couldn't do it. "Everything okay?"

He began to turn, but the tightness of her expression stopped him halfway.

"It's fine."

He set his jaw. He got her message. He got it loud and clear. "Great. Let's finish this."

They didn't stop again, just kept hauling themselves forward in grimly resolved silence. He could hear behind him the sounds of her beginning to tire—a sort of shuffle every other step or so. But he knew better than to ask how she was doing. She could confess her weakness of her own accord this time. He wasn't prying anything else out of her.

About midday they came to a boulder he'd been expecting, massive and split right in two so that half of it made a kind of mesa. They were close now.

He pulled out his phone and checked the GPS for the very first time that trip. Right on course.

She said nothing about him using the GPS. Finally, finally, he took a good look at her.

She was flushed, breathing at an increased pace, her hand braced against her bad leg—but her expression was open, if weary. Maybe she really was fine. Or maybe the possibility of getting to her plant was putting her in a better mood.

That thought put him into a fouler one. "We're close." He bit that off the way he'd tear off some jerky.

"You're still upset."

Jesus, did she have to sound like such a robot? "Nope. Just happy to be close to the end. Let's go."

Over the boulder they went, not even stopping to appreciate the view. Then over another rise, through a nasty ravine, and finally, there it was.

A small meadow, entirely clear of anything but a plant with small pink flowers. It was like a field of stars, only done in green and pink. No more than an acre, but what a beautiful sight.

This was why he came to the wilderness so often. For these rare, small moments of unutterable, indescribable grace.

She came to his side, and it took all his willpower to not reach for her hand. To not try to share this moment with her.

Her hand brushed his. Light, brief, but he had felt it. He

knew that it was the only contact she'd allow herself, even if she was craving it as badly as he was.

"I'm almost reluctant to cut any," she said after a while.

"You're not going to cut all of it, are you?"

"I don't think I'll need all of it to get five pounds." But the wonder had left her expression, which had taken on a mercenary edge. "I'm not going to cut it all," she said when she caught him watching her. "I'll take half, and if that isn't enough... Well, it isn't enough."

With that, she set to work getting supplies out of her pack. Some bags, sharp herb scissors—and a scale, just like he'd guessed. She went to work as if he weren't there, all her focus on her task.

She didn't ask for help and he didn't offer. He found a place to sit where he could watch her as she went *snip-snip-snip*. Jax came to sit with him, and Russ sank his hand into the fur at the dog's neck. Jax was going to need another clip soon. He looked more dignified with a long coat, but it was too hot here for that. Besides, the groomers loved Jax.

Russ set to work picking leaves and twigs and burrs out of Jax's fur and checking his paws for any foxtails. Jax closed his eyes and dozed, clearly enjoying the attention.

Bea snipped for one hour, then two, her focus so total it almost scared him. She didn't once look at him, and he knew it wasn't because she was trying to ignore him—she didn't look at anything else either. It was like watching someone meditate.

Bea stretched out to clip at a patch just out of reach, leg stretching behind her, ass lifting, the line of her neck bared to the sunlight.

Her neck. There was something about her neck...

No, not her neck. Someone else's.

Russ frowned. There was something he should be

remembering. A bell of memory his brain was ringing, trying to bring it to the surface.

He pulled out his phone, checked the signal. Nearly full strength. He could call the authorities and pull the curtain on all this. Maybe he should. She must be close to being done.

He didn't call up the keypad though. He just sighed as he stared at the phone screen. Jax nudged his nose under Russ's arm, crawling closer. Russ looked into Jax's mismatched eyes. "I've got to do it, buddy. It's my duty."

Jax raised a doggy eyebrow.

"Don't give me that look. They can't squat in a wilderness area. I agree that they're nice people, but they're still breaking the law," he said. "Wait, why are you sticking up for them? Their dogs wanted to kill you."

Jax dropped one eyebrow and raised the other.

"You're a better man than I," Russ said.

"Do you always talk to him?" Bea had finally stopped picking and was watching him.

"Sometimes. He's a good listener."

"I noticed that."

Russ had the suspicion she'd miss his dog more than she would him.

She went back to clipping, stretching out, baring her neck again—

Not her neck. Jake's neck.

Russ snapped up. "We have to go back."

The scissors went still in her hand. "Pardon?"

"We have to go back." Russ gestured toward his own neck. "He's got jugular venous distention."

"That still doesn't really explain anything."

"Shit. Why didn't I notice it right away? The shortness of breath, the coughing, the edema for crying out loud! And I saw his neck clear as day this morning and I didn't connect it…"

Because he'd argued with Bea. Because she didn't return his feelings and Russ was pouting like a spoiled brat—so he hadn't recognized the medical emergency in front of him.

"Jake's got congestive heart failure," he explained. "He's got all the signs. He needs to see a doctor. Right away."

For once, she didn't argue. "I was wondering what was wrong. But you can't make him see a doctor if he doesn't want to."

He stopped. She was right, but… "I can't do nothing."

Her gray eyes were clear and bracing. "Not everyone wants a hero."

You certainly didn't. "I can't let him die."

She frowned. "Do you think it's that serious?"

"If left untreated? Yes."

"Okay. Then how do we get him medical care?" She was so gravely practical it wrung his heart.

"I can call in the sheriff and Cal Fire and have them bring a medevac. In all the chaos of getting the camp cleared out, Jake will have to go with the medics." He nodded. Yes, that would probably work.

"So we'll destroy their life to get him treated."

She wasn't arguing with him, he realized—she was only examining all the sides. And that was an important one. "We were going to destroy their life anyway."

Her head drooped. "I know. I don't think I'm cut out for the superhero life."

"You let me worry about that. And keep playing devil's advocate. You're good at it."

A ghost of a smile flitted across her lips. "Perhaps you should be there when the authorities arrive, like you planned. Jake knows you and he seemed to like you—

perhaps if you explained things, he'd be more willing to go with the medics."

He chewed on that. "That's a good idea."

"But once you return, they'll know that the authorities are coming. They might run."

Their gazes held. "They might," he said deliberately.

"Ah." She understood instantly. "So you do split hairs."

"I'm not inflexible. And they are nice people. Even if they are breaking the law and causing a huge fire danger."

She smiled at him, small and sad, and he gave her one in kind. She brushed off her hands. "I'll go with you."

He frowned. "Wait. Do you have five pounds?"

"No. 3.68. But you can't go alone."

He pondered that. He could wait for her to finish, although it had taken her the better part of several hours so far. It would be dark before she was done. He couldn't hike down to the camp in the dark.

And if he sent the sheriff their way without any warning, they'd have no chance to escape.

"You came all this way for this very thing," he said. "And you want to pack up early?"

"You can't go alone. And if we can help Jake, we should." Her composure was reassuring. He was trained to make decisions in tough situations, to deal with stuff like this every day—but it was still nice to hear the calmness in her. The surety.

And nice to know that she cared enough to give up the rest of her blooms to help Jake. She might think she was cold, but she really wasn't. Not at all.

But— "There's no point in you coming along. There's nothing you can do."

Her face tilted back toward the flowers. "If you're sure." Her fingers tightened on the scissors. "Ash has a gun."

She thought she might protect him. Man, to have her think that... He cleared his throat hard. "I'm trained to deal with that. Once I call, I'll have backup too." He really wasn't being a hero here, not like she was thinking. "Ash is smart. She'll clear everyone out without a fuss." That's what he was counting on. As well as keeping Bea away from a possibly angry, gun-carrying hippie. She'd be safer here with Jax.

Her mouth pursed as if she was gearing up for another argument, but all she said was, "Please be safe."

"I will." He cleared his throat again, the hitch in it sticking hard. "You finish here. When it gets dark, put up the tent. I probably won't be able to come back until the morning, so just stay here where I can find you. You can manage on your own? Your phone is charged?"

She nodded without looking at him.

"I'll leave Jax too," he said. Jax gave him an inquiring look. "Stay here. Watch Bea." At Bea's name, Jax thumped his tail. "Good boy."

She did look at Jax then, her gaze unfocused. "He will. He'll take care of me."

Of course he would, because the dog already loved her. Russ grabbed his pack, then halted. "I'll have my phone, but I won't be able to use it there."

"I know," she said with a hint of a quaver.

He thought for a moment that she might rise and come to him. To do what though, he didn't know.

But she simply said, "You should hurry if you want to make it there before dark."

"Right." He turned away from her, his limbs oddly stiff, almost reluctant. "Stay," he said to Jax, not that the dog really needed it.

He marched off alone, their presence behind him a phantom weight that wouldn't dissipate.

Chapter 10

AS RUSS HAD EXPECTED, Ash met him at the entrance of the camp, shotgun in hand. She didn't look pleased to see him, but her frown wasn't threatening. It *was* still a frown.

"You forget something?"

Yeah, she definitely wasn't happy to see him. He wondered how best to approach this and then decided head-on would be best with her. "Jake is sick. You know that, don't you?"

Her eyes narrowed. "Anyone can tell that. And what's it to you?" There was a hint of fear beneath her pugnacity.

That fear gave him hope. "He's not just sick. It's congestive heart failure, and it's serious. Did you know *that*?"

"Again, what's it to you?" But she was beginning to understand, realization hardening in her expression.

"I care because it's my job to care. To help when I can."

She swallowed hard, showing uncertainty for the first time since she'd met her. "And what is your job?"

Time to blow everything up. "I'm a firefighter." He watched the gun in her grip like a hawk did a rabbit.

Her hand remained loose and the barrel never swung up. "Shit," she hissed. "Shit. Did you call the cops?"

He nodded, still watching the gun. Things could turn in an instant—he'd seen it happen before. "They're on their way," he admitted.

"Why are you telling us?" Ash slumped, the shotgun threatening to fall from her fingers. She wasn't going to fight this—she was admitting defeat.

"So no one gets hurt when they do arrive." *Please understand what I mean. Take those kids and get them out of here.* "Can you take me to Jake?"

Here was the next tricky bit. Ash might decide that Jake was coming with them, and he'd never get the medical attention he needed. Somehow Russ had to get her to leave a member of the group behind. And if he'd read Ash correctly, that was going to be tough.

Ash rubbed a rough hand along her jaw. "Are you sure he needs it now? Maybe it can wait until we're back in Mexico."

Russ shook his head. "Do you think I would have endangered myself if it wasn't serious?"

She smiled ruefully. "Yeah, I guess that is pretty ballsy. I thought you wanted to warn us too?"

Shades of Bea there, with the logic traps. Too bad things had to happen like this; he guessed Ash and Bea had more in common than they thought.

"That too. Please," he tried again. "Can you take me to Jake?"

Footsteps pounded from the camp, then Jilly came running toward them, wild-eyed, hair flying. Now *she* looked like she might go off. "What's going on?" The demand was high and fretful.

"They're coming," Ash said, calm as ever.

"Now? How did they find us?" Jilly took in Russ, the whites of her eyes showing. "Shit. It was you. Where is she? Your wife?"

A chill moved down his spine at the way she said it. "She's not my wife. And she's not here." Thank God. Bea was safe from whatever madness might go down here. Ash might have the gun, but Jilly was the one making him nervous.

"You tricked us," Jilly said, "just to turn us in!"

"No, we... We never meant to trick you." He held up his hands, trying to bring her down from her ramping hysteria. "Only to survive."

"And now you're destroying our life!"

He couldn't deny that. So he didn't.

"Be quiet," Ash said. "He only did what he had to. And he's giving us a chance here."

He sent Ash a grateful look, then put on his work face as he turned back to Jilly. Calm. Commanding. Trustworthy. "Jake needs medical attention."

Jilly's gaze darted from him to Ash and then back again, eyes more white than iris so panicked was she. "They're going to find the field."

Russ clenched his jaw. He'd just told her that her father was in danger, and she was worried about her pot? "Did you hear what I said?"

Ash gave him a small shake of her head before sending him an inquiring look. He nodded in answer. "They already know about the pot," she said to Jilly.

That completely set Jilly off. "We have to leave." She grabbed Ash's arm, the one holding the gun. "Now. Before they come."

"Jake needs medical attention," he repeated.

Ash shook her off. "Did you hear any of what he said?"

Jilly paid no attention. She took off at a run toward the camp.

Well, that was what he'd wanted: a chance for them to get away. Although Jake was her dad—Jilly might have shown a little more concern. Or any at all.

Never mind though; it was time to go help Jake. "Can you take me to him?"

Ash nodded. "Yeah. This way." She went toward the camp, motioning for him to follow.

"Aren't you going to run?"

She gave a jerky shrug. "I need to make sure Jake is okay. I've been worried about him, but..." Another jerky shrug from her and maybe even a sniffle? He couldn't quite tell. "Well, you're here and your friends are coming."

"We'll make sure he's taken care of."

Ash didn't respond to that, but he didn't hear any more of those suspicious sniffly noises either.

The camp was quiet when they came in, the tents still standing. But no kids or dogs came swarming to greet them.

So Jilly had run. He'd wanted her to, yet the sight of the empty camp filled Russ with unease. He hoped Jilly had left Jake like he'd asked.

Ash led them to the other side of the kitchen setup, toward a tent there. "Jake!"

"Over here." His voice was weak, devoid of breath. They found him in a chair, outside his tent. His lips were very lightly blue.

Russ knelt next to him and unslung his pack. "Hello, Jake."

"Jilly told me about you." But there was no hostility in

the man's voice. "Should have known you weren't an engineer."

"And how should you have known that?" Russ kept his tone upbeat and calm as began to take Jake's vitals. Not good.

"You don't move like an engineer," Jake said. Russ looked at him in surprise. Jake smiled. "But you're clearly crazy about that wife of yours."

Russ's stomach dropped. He didn't want to talk about Bea. "We've got help coming for you." Best to focus on what really mattered here.

"She's not his wife," Ash said.

Jesus. Russ clenched his jaw. Out of everything that had happened, Jake knowing that he and Bea had deceived everyone was the worst somehow.

"Oh?" Jake said, his breathing harsh. "But he's still crazy about her."

That was true. Even now, a corner of Russ's mind itched with the knowledge that Bea was alone with only Jax to protect her.

Rather than admit that yes, he was crazy about her, Russ said, "Okay, your vitals aren't great, but they're stable. A rescue team is on the way, and they'll get you to the hospital. Your condition is serious, but definitely treatable." Russ didn't like to think what would have happened to Jake if he hadn't finally put all the man's symptoms together. "Is all that clear?"

Jake nodded. "My brain's still getting enough oxygen. I think."

Russ couldn't help but smile. Jokes were a good sign. He looked up at Ash hovering over them. "How is Jilly getting out?"

"There's a truck we keep at the trailhead at the base of the mountain. She'll take that, drive into the valley." Yet more evasion from her.

"And you?"

She ignored him as she knelt next to Jake. "Russ will get you some help. I've been worried about you."

"Ash, you'll be arrested if you stay." Listen to him, helping someone evade the law. But he liked Ash—she reminded him of Bea. He guessed he just had the need to rescue everyone. No doubt Bea would have something incisive to say here about his superhero obsession.

Ash answered through a tight jaw. "I can't abandon Jake."

But his own daughter had, running like a rabbit when her skin was threatened.

"Ash." Jake had to struggle to get that out, his breathing growing erratic. "You should go. Russ'll take care of me, won't you, Russ?"

"And after you get out of the hospital?" She laid a hand on his forearm. "Jilly's halfway to the border by now. Someone's got to take care of you after."

Jake laid a hand over hers. "You can't do that if you're in jail."

Russ had to look away for a moment, so touched was he. He cleared his throat, looked back. "He's right."

"You turned us in." There was a flash of anger from Ash there.

"You know that I had to." It wasn't like he was happy about it.

She got to her feet. "I know. But I'm still pissed."

"Fair enough."

"I'll run now," she told Jake, "but once you're out of the hospital, you call my brother. You remember his number?"

Jake nodded.

"He'll let me know and I'll come get you. We'll go find Jilly and the kids in Mexico." She clasped Jake's shoulder before giving Russ an unfathomable look. "Will he be arrested?"

"I'll do my best." Russ would have to call in some favors, but it could be done, especially if Jake disavowed any knowledge of the pot operation.

"You make sure of that." For a moment she was the fierce, unapproachable Ash again, and then she turned and was gone.

Russ silently wished her good luck.

Jake stared after her for a long moment, looking wistful and a little lost. Then he asked, "So how long until your friends are here?"

"Cal Fire aren't my friends," he said lightly. "They call us the pavement princesses."

Jake laughed, then started coughing. And didn't stop.

Russ wished he had some oxygen to give him. That rescue team better be here soon.

He looked to the ridge near where Bea should be, although he couldn't see her. *Hang on, babe. I'll come rescue you next.*

But she didn't want him to rescue her. She only wanted her blooms and then to never see him again. Oh, she'd probably steal his dog if she could, but that was all she wanted from him.

"I'm sure she's fine," Jake said, some of his breath coming back to him. "Why'd you leave her behind?"

Good question. "Ash's gun." And Bea's obsession with that plant.

Jake pondered that, the rhythms of his breath falling

into something closer to normal. "You two aren't really married?"

"Nope."

"Wow. Could have fooled me."

They had fooled him. And maybe even Russ himself a bit. In the tent that night, things had felt... Well, never mind how they'd *felt*.

"Is she a firefighter?" Jake asked.

"No. I was only hired as her guide for a hiking trip up here. This was all a crazy accident." A perfect summation of every interaction he and Bea had shared.

Russ looked again toward the ridge where she ought to be, expecting again to see nothing.

Only... He narrowed his eyes. Was that—

A curl of smoke rose from the general area, growing thicker with each burst of wind.

"That marijuana field," he asked Jake, "would somebody torch it?" *Somebody* being either Jilly or Ash. *Don't let it be Ash.* If she'd set that fire after he let her escape...

So much for his superhero bona fides. Or even his honor as a firefighter.

Jake craned his neck, trying to see. "Oh no. Jilly—" His breath gave out. "Jilly said she might do that... if we were caught... but..."

But Jake didn't really believe his daughter capable of it. Or didn't want to believe.

"It wasn't Ash?" Probably not—the smoke column looked as if the fire had been set some time before Ash had taken off.

Jake shook his head. "Ash doesn't do stuff like that." He said nothing about Jilly—the resignation in his voice said it all for him.

Russ watched the column of smoke, took in the direction

and strength of the wind, studied the terrain. And came up with a chilling conclusion: That fire was going to go right toward Bea and Jax if it continued as it was.

He pulled out his phone—and saw he had no signal. "Fuck!" He almost, almost threw the phone into the dirt, so pissed was he. Of all the times to have no fucking signal...

"Is your wife up there?" Jake asked.

Russ didn't bother to correct him. "Yes, she is." Along with his dog. His professional façade cracked half an inch as panic fought its way out.

What could he do to save her?

He could stay with Jake until the authorities came and have them call in the fire. Or he could hike out of here until he found a spot where there was phone reception and call 911 himself. Jake would probably be fine on his own until someone came. Probably.

Or Russ could go save the girl.

Rushing into a fire without proper equipment and all on his own was stupid. Rushing into a brushfire like that was suicidal.

But Bea and Jax were in danger.

If he really were Superman, this was the point where he'd tear off his shirt to reveal the famous logo beneath. And then he'd fly off, save her and Jax, and put out the fire, all without breaking a sweat.

Russ wasn't Superman, or Batman, or Spider-Man, or any of the other heroes of his youth. He was a guy who was crazy about a woman who was in danger at that very moment—not to mention how he felt about Jax. But Russ was the closest thing to a superhero this situation had.

He set a hand on Jake's shoulder. "I need to go find Bea. The rescue team is on their way and they know where you are."

Jake waved toward the smoke. "Don't worry about me. Go save your lady."

Russ grinned, feeling surprisingly good even with the mess they were in. "I'm going to do just that. Whether she likes it or not."

Chapter 11

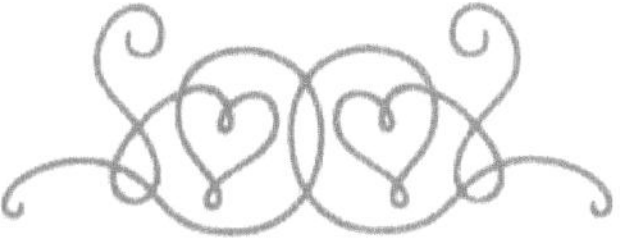

BEA CLIPPED ANOTHER BLOOM, CAREFUL not to crush it. She added it to the scale, holding her breath as the readout bounced around the final number, finally settling on 4.998lbs.

The air burned her throat as she released it from her tight lungs. She'd done it. After everything she'd been through, she had her penstemon.

With utmost caution, she put the blooms into the sacking she'd brought, gently, lovingly wrapping them for the trip back. When she was finished, she looked over at Jax, waiting patiently with his head on his paws.

"We're done," she called to him. She felt less alone talking to him, although he was a poor substitute for Russ no matter how awesome he was. "It's all over."

Jax had nothing to offer to that, not even a cock of his ear.

"It's finished," she tried a final time.

That had him raising his head. Then dropping it again.

"No, it doesn't really make me feel any better either. Strange, isn't it?"

But Russ was right; talking to Jax was soothing, even if the dog couldn't respond verbally.

She put the last bag of blooms into her pack and zipped it shut. No, that didn't make her feel any better either. She had exactly what she'd come for, and she felt terrible.

When she sighed, Jax belly-crawled over to her and set his head on her thigh. She reached out to rub his ears. Yes, that did help.

Might as well get some other stuff done while she waited for night to fall, because waiting for Russ would probably be useless. She pulled out her phone, called up her e-mail. There was a message from her lab manager telling her the repairs wouldn't start for another week—which stunk, but there was nothing to be done. Then another e-mail from Kelly saying that Bea's suggestion hadn't worked and what was she supposed to do now? Bea sent a reply, trying to talk Kelly down and reminding the student they'd meet soon. Finally she sent an e-mail addressed to the entire lab: *I got the blooms, all five pounds. Start prepping for the extraction and purification.*

Nothing showy or bragging or even exultant. That wasn't Bea's style. But her lab would understand what this meant— they would provide the excitement all on their own.

She hit Send, waited for a sense of... something, anything to come over her. But nothing came. All this effort to get these plants and she was only drained in the end.

But she couldn't simply sit and stare off at nothing— time to get on with setting up the tent. The sun was half gone already, and in about two hours it would be dark. She hoped Russ would back before then, but it seemed unlikely. There wasn't enough time for him to get to the camp, settle things there, and hike back to her. He might not even come himself—he might send one of the rangers or sheriffs or whoever showed up to come get her. It wasn't as if he personally had to come fetch her.

She got to her feet, her knees creaking in protest at the change in position. She'd spent too many hours crouched over in this field. But she hadn't even noticed the discomfort in her joints, which was usual for her. When she was focused on her work, everything else fell away. Another thing the men in her life found hard to swallow.

The hike out was going to be miserable. For many reasons.

She lifted her pack and made her way to the pile of equipment at the edge of the field. Jax came trotting at her heels, his head and tail down.

"I know just how you feel. It's going to be a long, cold night." She began to haul the tent out, her shoulders twinging as she did, protesting yet more work.

Something acrid tickled at her nose, and she stopped dead. She sniffed the air, tested it. Was that smoke? She sniffed again, all of her still as she tried to sort through the smells coming through.

Perhaps it was. She took one more breath. This time there was no mistake as her nose burned with the odor of ash and heat.

She spun, looking for the source, her gaze searching, searching, searching as her heart took up a drumbeat in her ears.

There, down the mountain, was a growing plume of black smoke. Where was that? And how far?

She squinted at the smoke, her brain trying to calculate. Judging the distance of the fire was almost impossible from here, the thick scrub obscuring exactly where it was located—but she could tell which way the wind was blowing.

Northwest. Which meant that wind was going to push the fire right at her and Jax.

The dog whined and sidled closer to her, no doubt smelling the smoke too.

"Change of plans," she said. "We're getting out of here. But first, let's call for some help."

Russ's phone probably wasn't working, but hers was. Her hands were only slightly trembling as she called up her GPS, memorized the coordinates, and then dialed 911.

"Nine one one. What's your emergency?" the dispatcher asked with calming briskness.

"I'm in the San Jacinto Wilderness Area and there's a brush fire." Maybe Bea wasn't quite as calm as the dispatcher.

The operator took the information from her, including her location, and then asked, "Can you get to safety?"

"Well..." Bea wondered how to explain the situation. "I'm here with a firefighter. I think he might have called for the sheriffs a while ago."

If Russ hadn't, she might have just gotten him into trouble.

She heard the operator typing into a computer. "Oh, yeah. I see the call here. Illegal encampment and medical emergency. But there's nothing here about a fire."

"Are they there yet? He's at the encampment and they don't have cell service."

"I'm not sure," the operator said. "But the important thing is can you get to safety?"

Bea pondered that. She was alone with only a dog for company, with a fire coming toward her. Daunting didn't quite cover it.

She looked again toward the smoke, which was darker, more looming. Coming closer.

A shiver took hold but she shook it off. No, she could do it. It would be frightening and difficult, but she could do it.

But how to get to safety? If she tried for the trailhead they'd come in on, she'd pass directly in the fire's path. Not to mention the landslide blocking the trail and the two days it would take to get back. Darkness was coming—she had to be careful where she ended up when it fell.

There was the camp. Russ was there, but again, that put her in the fire's path if she took the most direct route. But perhaps she could go north for a ways, then turn east to get back to the camp. She tested the wind again, studying the way it moved her hair. The wind was blowing more west than north. If it kept on like that, the fire would head straight up the mountain.

"Yes," she told the operator. "I'll head to the encampment and meet the emergency personnel there." Much more confident than she felt.

"I'll hang up then," the operator said, "to preserve your phone battery. And rescue personnel will be informed that you're in the area and heading to the encampment."

"Thank you," Bea said and then hung up. "We can rescue ourselves, can't we Jax?"

He raised a doggy eyebrow, neither confirming nor denying.

"You're right—we need to get moving." She dropped her pack and began unloading anything nonessential. The less she carried, the faster she could move. Clothes, the spare tent, her scale, and the hot chocolate were all left behind— the flowers she kept. She silently asked forgiveness for littering like this. But she found a headlamp, which would come in very handy.

When she was done, the smell of smoke was stronger,

the column rising into the sky much thicker and darker. And blowing toward her.

"Ready?" she asked Jax.

He only watched with his mismatched eyes. But it was close enough to a yes.

She headed straight north at first, through rough, untamed terrain. Her leg ached like a bastard, and even Jax was panting hard, his sides heaving.

"Sorry, buddy. I'd go slower, but I don't want to die."

Jax didn't say anything, but she guessed he probably agreed with that.

Every so often she looked back at the column of smoke, unable to tell if it was getting bigger or coming closer. It certainly wasn't going away and she hadn't heard any emergency personnel, so she pushed on. And on and on, until she came to a canyon.

Too deep to climb through, much too wide to jump—there was no way around. At least not as far as she could tell. She'd turned on her headlamp, but night was falling and fast—it was impossible to see more than a few feet in front of her.

Apparently this was nature's way of telling her it was time to head east and down the mountain. She began to make her way down a steep face, keeping the canyon on her left and clutching at whatever she could to keep from sliding straight off the mountain.

"Worst camping trip ever," she muttered. "Jax! You still with me?"

A wet nose brushed her hand.

"All right, I think a trail should be coming up soon." She was more praying that the trail was coming up soon, to be honest.

Down, down, down they went, the few feet of space illuminated by the headlamp the only thing that seemed real in the darkness surrounding them. Bea had no idea what the fire was doing; she saw no glow from it but could still smell smoke. The night was immensely quiet yet also incredibly loud, every errant sound a drumbeat against her ears and heart.

Frankly, it was terrifying. But Russ was out there somewhere, a bright spot just beyond the beam of the headlamp, and she meant to reach him.

To keep track of the time and avoid checking her phone every other minute and killing the battery, she began to count her steps. When she got to sixty, she started all over, keeping count of how many times she got to sixty. When she got to ten rounds, she felt as if she had been going for an hour.

When she got to thirty rounds, she let herself cry a bit. Anyone might have cried out there, alone except for the world's most amazing dog. Anyone.

When she got to forty, she briefly contemplated simply sitting down where she was. It was a flattish area, and she could set up a tent or at least take a rest. But the smoke coating her nose kept her moving on.

That and the bright spot that was Russ, who had to be out there looking for her. She couldn't disappoint him by not looking for him.

When she got to forty-eight, she heard a voice. A human voice.

"Here! I'm here!" She didn't even know where *here* was, but she yelled it with all her might.

A pause, a hanging pause that made her throat close, and then so, so faintly, "Bea!"

Russ. He'd found her.

"I'm here," she called again. "Where are you?"

"Bea!" Faint still—she didn't think he'd heard her. But he was below her; she could hear that.

Jax barked.

"Yes, yes," she encouraged the dog. "He'll hear you before he hears me. Bark!"

Jax merely stared at her.

"Oh, um, no... Speak!"

And Jax barked. Sharp and short and the sweetest sound she'd ever heard.

"Good dog, you are such a good dog. Speak!"

She made her way down the hill, yelling at Jax to speak, skidding part of the way. And then skidding more of the way.

And then straight-out sliding down the hill on her butt, her heels digging into the dirt, with no control over her speed. Jax ran at her side, barking his head off.

Her butt left the ground and caught air in a sickening reminder of how she'd hurt her leg. She began to fall, bracing for the hard ground about to hit her—

And she was caught by a very sturdy, very familiar set of arms.

"Jesus Christ, Bea. Are you trying to kill me?"

Oh, his voice. She was so happy to hear it she wrapped her arms around his neck and pressed her face into his chest. She was safe. He'd found her.

His arms tightened around her, and his chest rose and fell in sawing breaths against her cheek.

"Oh God, I didn't think I'd find you and there was the fire and—" She kissed him then, because she was so happy to see him. He kissed her back just as fiercely, relief and heat and happiness flowing between them.

"The fire?" she asked when they were done.

He took a moment to answer, his chin resting on her hair. "Put out, thanks to you."

That *was* good news. "And Jake?"

"On his way to the hospital in Palm Springs." There was a vibration deep in his voice. Almost a fissure.

"And the camp?" She swung her gaze up to his face, trying to find the source of that fissure in his expression.

He switched off her headlamp. "Sorry. It was blinding me." She couldn't see him at all now. "Ash stayed and helped me with Jake as long as she could. She left before the sheriff came. She'll meet up with Jake once he's out of the hospital."

"Ash? But why not Jilly? That's her father."

"Jilly ran off as soon as I showed up. Took the kids."

Bea bit her lip. She hadn't gotten a deep impression of Jilly in their time together, but Bea never would have guessed she'd do that. "Will they be all right?" By *they* she really meant the kids. Jilly could fend for herself.

"Ash said they have a truck hidden at the base of the mountains and that they'll probably head to Mexico."

"Oh." There was nothing too objectionable there—they had been hoping the kids would be able to leave before the SWAT team showed—but the unease wouldn't dissipate. "I suppose she and the kids are all right."

"Probably." His tone was grudging. Perhaps he shared her unease. Or perhaps he regretted giving them the chance to escape. But there had been clear approval in his voice when he'd spoken of Ash and Jake.

But all was well that ended well. Or at least mostly well. "Thank God you'd already called for rescue when that fire started," she said. "Otherwise it could have been very, very bad."

"That fire didn't start by accident." Rage smoldered under the words. "Jilly set fire to the marijuana field."

"Oh God." Bea clapped a hand to her mouth as her heart kicked against her chest. Jilly had endangered everyone simply to cover her tracks. And not even very well—Russ and Bea knew about the field and could tell everyone no matter what.

"Yeah. If she didn't have those kids, I'd haul her off to jail myself. As it is, the sheriff has a description of her."

Bea didn't want to think of what would happen to the kids if Jilly went to jail, but she had to admit the woman would deserve it. "And Ash?"

"They don't have a very good description of Ash, no."

So he had tried to save Ash too. Rather against his super-hero ideals, but he'd done it. She wasn't quite certain what to say after that.

He spoke again before she could find something to say. "I'll take you to the rescue team. They'll get you out of here."

You. Not *us.* He wasn't going with her.

"Oh. Thank you." Her throat closed and her nose burned, but no tears came. Really, she should have expected that. His job here was over—she had her plants and someone else could take her off the mountain. "Jax is very happy to see you."

An inane comment, but one that put a buffer between them.

"I'm glad to see him." Russ raised the flashlight in his hand and started off, still carrying her.

"You should put me down. I can walk, and I don't want you to fall in the dark and break your neck."

He said nothing, just kept on.

"Please. Please put me down." It was killing her, the

thought of him carrying her to safety when she knew she'd just have to say good-bye right away.

"Bea." His commanding tone was back. "Just let me rescue you. I know you don't need it, but just this once let me do it."

So she let him, because she knew it was important to him, living up to his idea of a hero. And because it would be the last time.

Chapter 12

BEA POKED AT THE IV line snaking around her arm, not daring to touch the needle itself.

"When did they say I could leave again?"

Her cousin Luke paused in unpacking the bag he'd brought, his half-healed black eye a rainbow ring of bruises. "The nurse said she'd be back to remove that IV and then you can go."

No timeline then. Depending on how busy the ER was, Bea could be here another ten minutes or an hour. She knew the drill. Of course, she could always pull the line out herself... She shuddered at the thought. No, she was going to wait.

"Fee's on her way," Luke said. "And Benedict's retrieving your car."

Once Bea and Russ had come upon the rescue team, she'd been bundled onto the back of an ATV and taken out of the wilderness, then bundled into an ambulance and taken to an ER in Palm Springs. No one listened when she'd said she was fine. Russ had said nothing as she was taken away—he'd been pulled aside by the sheriff who looked to be in charge.

She had gotten to give Jax a pat good-bye though. So there was that.

"Did Russ call you?" Her roundabout way of asking if Luke had heard from Russ.

"Uh, no, the sheriff did. Or, he called Lil and Lil called me."

"How is Lil?" Bea wouldn't have stressed her cousin for the world, but it was too late now. She could only hope Lil wasn't too freaked out.

"Climbing the walls. I think that Brazilian is holding her down on the couch."

Luke didn't like Adriano, or *that Brazilian* as he called him. Bea had met Adriano the once and hadn't been impressed herself. He'd been positively surly. Russ never would have behaved like Adriano had.

Stop it.

"But she's okay?" Bea asked.

"Yeah, she's fine. You should call and let her know you're okay. I don't think my text reassured her." He shoved a few more things into the bag, not bothering to be gentle about it.

"I will once I'm out of here." She briefly considered asking him how he'd gotten the black eye—her curiosity was burning a hole into her stomach—but since he hadn't explained it at the very beginning, he wasn't likely to answer now. Which meant it probably had something to do with a woman.

Which made her that much more curious.

Luke paused, wrapping a phone-charger cord around his hand before slowly unwinding it, then winding it round again. "This is probably going to upset you to talk about, but Lil told me what happened between you and Russ."

Bea felt her lungs turn to iron. *How did they*—But Luke was only talking about the blind date. Neither he nor Lil knew about what happened in the mountains. Still, she couldn't quite think of how to respond.

"I'm so sorry," Luke went on. "If I'd known, I never would have asked Russ to take you. I know how you are about that stuff and how... how upset you must have been to see him. All I can say is that I'm sorry." He wouldn't meet her gaze.

"It's okay. You didn't know." The IV suddenly itched like mad, but she couldn't touch it. Where was that nurse?

"Yeah, but after Lil explained everything—"

"Explained what?" a voice burst in.

Fee waited in the doorway. Her younger sister had her eyes—cool gray eyes, Spencer eyes—but her hair was a rich brown to Bea's black and held a wave. She was shorter, curvier—all in all a warmer, more welcoming version of Bea. Except right now Fee had a pretty confrontational look on her face.

"Are you all right?" Fee demanded, as if Bea were responsible for all this.

Bea felt herself shutting down. Sometimes Fee triggered that in her, a need to shrink away from her sister's hard-charging personality. "I'm fine. Just banged up my leg."

"Then why are you still here? Shouldn't they have discharged you by now?"

Bea knew exactly how irritating she could be to people because Fee very often behaved as Bea did—and Bea found her sister's behavior immensely irritating at times. Like right now.

"We're waiting for the nurse to take out my IV." She held up her arm.

Fee peered at it. "You could probably take it out yourself."

Bea cupped a protective hand over it. "I'm not that kind of doctor."

Fee made a noise that could have been acceptance or disgust. "So, what did Lil need to explain?"

Luke looked embarrassed as he glanced at Bea. But he kept his mouth shut.

Bea rubbed her fingertips against her temples. Fee could be like a terrier when she sank her teeth into something. But Luke already knew and so did Lil—what did it matter if Fee knew? They weren't a gossipy family, not really, but stories did spread.

"Luke asked a friend of his to be my guide on this hiking trip," Bea said, her voice remarkably calm. "What he didn't know was that this... *friend* and I had a blind date a few months ago." It sounded so innocuous, so tame—yet the emotions boiling up in Bea were anything but.

"So?" Of course Fee didn't understand. Neither had Lil. Which meant that the problem was entirely Bea's. Not that knowing that helped.

"Look," said Luke, straightening up from plugging in Bea's dead phone. "Bea didn't want to spend a weekend alone with the guy."

Bea's cheeks went hot. Okay, so maybe Luke understood.

Fee gave the smallest of eye rolls. "I get that."

"I don't think you do," Luke said warningly. Perhaps to protect Bea, perhaps to assuage his own guilt.

"There's more," Bea said. Might as well get it all out. "I slept with him on the date. And on this trip."

The discomfort that burned through Bea was almost worth it to see Fee's mouth drop. Luke averted his face, his eyes half closing as if he wanted to unhear that.

"Okay," said Fee slowly. "That's... I wasn't expecting that."

"Well, that's why Luke was apologizing for asking Russ to go with me," Bea said stiffly. "He didn't know."

"I don't see why he should apologize to you because you slept with a man."

Luke gave a strained laugh. "Well, I was." He slapped his palms on his thighs. "Okay, everyone knows everything, and everyone's apologized for everything. And again, I'm sorry. I know how tough that trip must have been for you, Bea. So now we can drop it."

As he said it, Bea realized that while she was embarrassed to admit everything that had happened with Russ, the world hadn't ended. This then was the difference between your family seeing your failures versus the entire world—yes, it was difficult, but in the end, it was fine. She was fine.

"It's all right," she told Luke again. "I'm no wilting flower." She'd hiked miles on an injured leg, pretended to be married to keep from being shot, and run away from a wildfire. That was almost close to superheroine status. "Speaking of flowers, where's my pack?"

Luke pointed to a spot next to the chair in the room. "Right there. Did you get what you needed?"

"Yep."

"That's good, since the field might have burned."

She grabbed her stomach. "What?"

"They can't just tell yet, but it's likely that the fire went over your field of flowers."

"That—" Bea wouldn't have called herself bloodthirsty, but she found herself wishing the police would catch Jilly and that the woman got her just punishment. Although that would hurt the kids.

But her plant... "The nightshade penstemon might be entirely gone." Her stomach rolled beneath her palm. If the compound did have promising properties, that promise would be useless if they couldn't get more of it. "Who told you this?"

"I called Russ on the way over."

So he had talked to Russ. She was dying to know what he'd said, what they'd spoken of, if she had come up beyond her condition in the hospital—but she kept her mouth shut.

Luke went to the door and poked his head out. "Where's that nurse?"

Fee came over and sat on the bed next to Bea. "I called Mom and Dad. You'll need to call and tell them you're fine."

"Why did you do that?" Of all the high-handed things... "I was going to call them after. Now they're worried when they don't have to be." Really, Fee could have stopped to think before barging in.

Fee shrugged. "You can call them on the way home."

That was another irritating aspect of Fee—she tended to take over, to take charge, without even considering what others might want, but it wasn't worth fighting over.

Bea's phone buzzed then, the battery coming back to life. She climbed off the bed, careful of the IV, and grabbed the phone, the familiar shape a comfort in her hand. There was a text from her parents—she quickly typed out that she was fine and would call later. Another from Lil—Bea sent pretty much the same message she'd sent to her parents. One from Benedict saying he'd retrieved her car—she told him thank you.

Then she called up her e-mail. Nothing from Kelly—perhaps the poor girl had given up for the weekend. But there was a message from Stan, a postdoc in her lab with the message line: GREAT NEWS!!!!

She did not want to open that, not with what might be the very last of the nightshade penstemon in her pack and the rest burned to ash somewhere on the mountain. It suddenly seemed obscene to do experiments with a plant that might be extinct.

But that was silly—she was the head of the lab and she had to lead. So she opened it.

And put a hand to her heart, which threatened to jump from her chest.

It couldn't be... She read it again, thinking her brain had scrambled the letters into what she'd wanted to see rather than the words that were actually there. But no, it stayed the same.

Got the plant to grow in the lab—twenty shoots popped up this morning, looking strong. Already contacted botany dept. Also, the chemists tell me they finally managed to synthesize the compound—figured out the process just this weekend. So we've got the plant to grow and a way to synthesize the compound. Isn't that awesome?!!

The penstemon wasn't extinct. Not that they even needed it now, not if the chemical synthesis was working.

But this trip had been an utter waste. The burned field, the ruined camp, Ash and Jilly and Jake and the kids all scattered... and Russ and Jax and her, entangled and separated again... All of it for nothing. Utterly and completely nothing.

She put her head into her hands, her eyes burning as tears slipped from them.

"Bea?" Fee put a hand at her back. "Are you okay?"

Bea took a choking, shuddering breath, trying to beat back the tears. "Where's the nurse? Tell him to get in here or I'm pulling this stupid thing out myself."

"Sure." Fee patted her back as if comforting a child. "Sure."

Bea slapped the phone back onto the counter, switching the screen to black. "Tell them I'm ready to go home."

RUSS DREW patterns on the bar top with the condensation on his beer bottle, circle overlapping circles, until he'd come up with something like a flower.

But not like a penstemon bloom. Penstemon was much prettier than what he'd just made.

Luke walked up, pulled out the stool next to him, and sat down. "Hey."

Neither met the other's gaze.

"Hey." If Russ had been hoping this wouldn't be awkward, he was wrong.

It had been a week since the camping trip. A week where he hadn't tried to contact Bea, where she hadn't contacted him. Here with Luke he'd get his first real news of her. Not just that she'd left the hospital with a clean bill of health, but how she was *really* doing.

"About that hiking trip—" he started.

Luke cleared his throat hard. "Bea told me what happened. All of it. Both before and after." He didn't sound happy about it.

"Wait? *Bea* told you?" Russ would have thought Bea would take that secret to the grave. It seemed she was different with her family.

She hadn't told any of them about the blind date before—but she'd confessed all after the hiking trip. Which meant... Russ wasn't quite sure what it meant, but maybe there was some hope in that news.

"Yeah," Luke said.

The heaviness of that told Russ that Luke didn't want to discuss it further. Fine with Russ. He had to think on this information.

"How is she?"

"She's... well," Luke said, "but she doesn't really confide in me. That's more Lil's thing. But Lil's been sick with this pregnancy. Bea's come by most days this week to check on her." He peeled off part of the bottle label. "I guess the best way to describe her is a little sad."

"Oh." Maybe she was missing Jax. The dog was definitely missing her—*a little sad* described Jax this week too. "Did she...?"

"She hasn't really mentioned you."

"Oh." That said it all, didn't it? He started a new condensation flower. "How's her leg?"

"Fine, I suppose."

And there it was—the end of what Russ could ask about Bea. She was fine—if a little sad—her leg was fine, and she hadn't mentioned him. The conversation was done. At least that part of it.

"I am really sorry about what happened. All of it." If they were done, Russ had to get that bit in. He was sorry their blind date had gone so wrong, that the hiking trip had gone even worse, that he couldn't protect Bea from everything that had happened... all of it.

Luke shrugged. "If I'd known about the blind date, I never would have suggested this. So it's partly my fault. And it's nobody's fault that you guys ran into those hippies out there. Did they ever find the woman who set the fire?"

Russ shook his head. Jake had been released from the hospital with a medication regimen to keep him healthy. Russ hadn't seen it for himself, but one of the nurses had said that a middle-aged woman with dirty-blond hair had come to get him.

That would be something to tell Bea if she ever called. Or if he ever worked up the nerve to call her. Maybe he could send an e-mail, include some pictures of Jax. That was kind of a dirty tactic though. The all's fair in love and war thing didn't include dogs.

"Well, no one got hurt, and the fire never got too big," Luke said philosophically. "And Bea's plant is growing now in the lab, so she won't ever need to go harvest it again."

"Good for her," Russ said, because it was the proper thing to say next and not because he believed it.

"Yeah, it will be. Bea's never really done well outside her comfort zone."

That brought Russ up short. "What do you mean? She was amazing in some tough circumstances." No wonder she thought she couldn't handle new things if her family kept telling her she couldn't.

"Come on." Luke gestured with his beer. "She's my cousin and I love her dearly, but you've seen what she's like."

Russ faced Luke and squared his shoulders. "Yeah, I have seen what she's like, and she's awesome. So I suggest you stop saying shit like that."

"What the fuck?" Luke came off the barstool. "She's my fucking cousin."

"And she's my…"

What, girlfriend? Nope and nope. *Lover?* Not true and also dated. *Friend?* They had agreed to leave as friends, but that was a Band-Aid over the whole situation.

No, they weren't friends either.

"Dude." Luke sat back down heavily and pushed his beer away. "What exactly happened out there?"

Russ's shoulders slumped. "Didn't Bea tell you?"

"She told me you slept together, but that was about it."

So Bea hadn't really told her cousin anything, because there was so much more than the night they'd spent together. Russ filled his lungs, tried to clear his mind. "Okay, we've got to start with the date. This woman bid on me at a charity bachelor auction but sent me over to Bea's as a joke, I guess. I was never really clear on that."

Luke frowned. "I can't imagine Bea was happy to see you on her doorstep."

"She wasn't at first. But man, she had this look on her face like she was daring me to convince her." Russ stared at his bottle as he recalled that look of hers. "And I know she's your cousin, but you have to know that she's smoking hot."

"Okay, we can never mention that part again."

Russ shrugged. "Sorry. Anyway, we went out, had a great time, and she got drunk. Not sloppy drunk, but definitely feeling it. And definitely aware of herself and what she was doing." He didn't want Luke to think he'd taken advantage of her. "I fell asleep that night thinking how awesome it had been and how much I was looking forward to taking her to brunch the next day. And doing it all over again next weekend. But when I woke up, she'd already left. So I waited for her to call, figuring I'd give her a little space to figure things out. And she never did."

He'd finished another condensation flower, this one more ragged than the first. His beer was getting warm.

"That all sounds remarkably like Bea," Luke said. "Except going out with you in the first place and getting drunk and going to your place."

"Well, she did. Then we met at the trailhead and she was... she was clearly anxious about going on the trip with me. But we were doing fine, except for her leg. And then we found that marijuana field and..." God, what he was about to say sounded so damn stupid. "We had to pretend to be married to survive."

Luke blinked at him. "What. The. Fuck?"

"Just go with it. So we're pretending to be married, and we're so good at it that it felt almost like we were married. Or that we should be. I pointed this out to Bea, and that maybe we should try a relationship once we were out of *Deliverance*-land—and she said no."

"Wait." Luke set a hand on the bar top as if to stop time. "Go back. Bea pretended to be married to you? And people bought it?"

"Are you shocked because I'm in the equation"—Russ pointed to himself—"or that Bea even tried to pretend at all?"

"You're a stand-up guy. I wouldn't have sent you off alone in the wilderness with my cousin if you weren't." Luke shook his head. "No, it's Bea pretending. I don't even think she pretended as a kid."

"Of course she did," Russ said. Luke did seem to love his cousin, but man, did he insist on putting her into a narrowly defined box.

"Maybe she did, but she definitely doesn't now." Luke took a pull from his beer. "I don't even think she reads fiction."

Luke really had no idea that Little Miss Scientist was a raging fan of gore and ice zombies and dragons. Couldn't get more fictional than that.

"She does pretend, and she's great at it. But when I told her there was something more between us, she said..."

I'll never come to you.

Suddenly it all became clear to Russ. He was doing the same damn thing as before and expecting different results.

And so was she. So much for them being rational individuals.

Time for something different then. But what?

Something very, very irrational occurred to him. Something spectacularly irrational. Something that would leave Bea with no doubts about how he felt about her—crazy.

He tapped the bottle against the bar, the glass chiming. It was a risk. She was just as likely to tell him off as to kiss him senseless if he did what he was planning.

But if she liked it, then maybe... maybe this something between them could grow. In a more normal situation, without being stranded in the wilderness or coming across an illegal encampment.

But still with the occasional hot pot and karaoke. They both enjoyed that.

"What? What did she say?" Luke asked.

"Never mind what she said." That message was just for Russ. "Do you think you could help me plan something?"

"That sounds... dangerous." But Luke didn't sound too reluctant.

"Nope, not a bit of danger. And if it all goes south, I won't tell Bea you were involved."

"Okay, now it really sounds dangerous. Bea doesn't like surprises."

"Yes, she does. You guys have convinced her that she doesn't." If she did agree to go out with him, Russ was going to have to work on that with her.

"Hey, I think I know her better than you," Luke said. "How do you know she likes surprises?"

"Because I surprised her on that date and she loved it. She just won't show it." Another thing he'd have to work on with her. Or he'd just have to become better at reading her.

"Dude, I am so going to regret this. Look, you've got to

tell me what you're thinking, and if it's too much, I'm going to veto it."

Quickly Russ sketched out his plan.

Luke listened, openmouthed. "That's crazy."

"Yeah, but I'm crazy about her and I want to prove it."

I'm coming to you, Bea. Get ready.

"It will certainly prove you're crazy. It's a lot, but I guess it's not too much." Luke didn't sound all that convinced though.

"Well, if she answers no, we'll know it was too much. Come on, Luke—she's way more daring than you guys give her credit for."

Luke pondered that. "Okay. But what do you need from me?"

"I need you to get something from Lil without arousing her suspicion. Or Bea's."

Luke snorted. "You don't ask for much, do you?"

"Can you do it?"

"Hell yes. What do you need?"

Russ leaned in and told Luke exactly what he'd require for his crazy, spectacular spectacle.

Chapter 13

BEA HIT SEND ON E-MAIL number one thousand and one for the day, then checked the time. Fifteen minutes until her Intro to Cell Biology class started. She gathered up the day's notes, checked that she had some markers and an eraser since they were never any at the whiteboard, and stuffed them into her messenger bag.

Before she left, she checked the pot in the windowsill holding the penstemon shoot. The others had been given to the botany department and would be replanted in the mountains when they were big enough, but she'd asked to keep this one. It seemed to be doing well, even so far from where it should be, as it reached two tiny leaves toward the sunlight.

She touched a finger to the pot, the clay cold and rough to the touch. She'd thought for so long that the plant would never thrive so far from home, yet here it was, doing just fine. If it wasn't thriving, it was at least doing its damnedest to.

She dug into her bag and pulled out her phone, pondering the half-formed resolution taking shape in her mind. She rubbed her thumb along the phone's edge, as cold as the pot had been, but smooth instead.

In the week since they'd come back, she'd thought and thought on what Russ had said. On their last disagreement. She wouldn't call it a fight—it was too calm for that. He'd been right—she'd pushed him away because she was frightened. She could unwind with her family, with her longtime friends, because they knew her, warts and all, and still loved her.

But she was afraid that if she relaxed like that with Russ, he would realize that he didn't like her. That warts-and-all Bea was too much even for a man who wanted to see the good in everyone. Which absolutely terrified her.

Better to give him the prickly, pushy, unapproachable Bea and see his turning away as a natural response to that than to give him the soft, vulnerable Bea and have him reject her anyway.

But that reasoning didn't *feel* right. It felt false. More fake than their "marriage." So perhaps it was time to trust her gut and reject it.

She pulled up a new text message, entered in Russ's info. She pulled a deep breath. She could do this. It wasn't so scary.

I will never come to you. And yet she was about to do just that.

Before her nerve could fail, she typed in: *Maybe you might like to get some hot pot this Friday?*

She hit Send and immediately regretted it. That sounded stupid and curt. She should have asked more nicely. She should have asked how he was doing, or put in something about how only if he were free, and if he didn't want to, it was no big deal, and now he'd feel obligated even if he didn't want to—

She shut the phone off, preventing her from sending anything else. And preventing her from having to read any response of his until after her class. Or whenever she chose to turn the phone back on. Convenient that.

The phone went back into her bag as she squared her shoulders and willed those butterflies in her stomach out. Time for class.

She crossed campus at a fast clip, trying to make up time, her phone a thumping weight in her bag as it slapped against her hip. But the phone kept quiet, just as she'd meant it to.

When she arrived in the lecture hall, it was already half-full. A few students smiled at her, but most ignored her. She wouldn't become real to them until she began the lecture, she knew.

At five after she began, falling into the familiar posture and rhythms of teaching. "All right, everyone. Did you all see the required reading on the website? Have that done by next class meeting—we'll cover it next time and you'll go into detail with it in your sections. Today we'll continue our discussion of G-protein-coupled receptors—"

The fire alarm began to squeal.

Bea jumped and bit back her instinctive curse. Why did the fire alarm always have to go off at the most inopportune moment? She was already behind in her lecture schedule for the quarter.

The students were looking around, waiting for someone to be the first to evacuate. God forbid any of them take the initiative.

She dropped her markers into her bag—she wasn't losing those—then clapped her hands to get their attention. "All right, gather your things and let's exit calmly." They weren't supposed to grab anything, just to get out, but she knew that was nonsense.

She was tucking her notes into her messenger bag when she heard the tramp of heavy boots coming down the lecture-hall stairs. And eddies of frightened whispers swirling through the students. What was going on—?

Russ.

When she looked up, Russ was marching toward her in his uniform—no, turnouts—with his "you must obey me" expression on his face.

She could only stare, openmouthed and too stunned to speak, as he came for her. He was here. And looking too damn good to be true.

When he hoisted her up into his arms, she found enough voice to give an indignant squeak. *Everyone was watching*—how would she regain her professorial authority after this? The students would want all kinds of assignment extensions and grade changes after this.

Russ swung around to face the room and she buried her face in her hands, her cheeks hot against her palms. "Shouldn't you all be evacuating?" he asked in his commanding voice.

Even though she wanted the earth to swallow her, her pulse still jumped at that tone of his.

"Is this a drill?" one student asked.

"Yep. But you still need to be evacuating."

"What are you doing with Professor Schuler?"

Oh, brave little undergrad to ask that. Bea would like to know herself. At least beyond igniting a mixture of discomfort and lust that threatened to make her spontaneously combust. Although if she did, there was a firefighter close at hand.

"I'm rescuing her," Russ said simply.

She let her hands fall from her face and stared up at him. She could stop this now, simply push against his chest and tell him to let her down. He would do it, she knew.

But she also knew it was important to him to be the hero. Not just to play the hero, but to *be* one. If she wanted him to accept her as the prickly, difficult person she was, she had to accept his open, friendly, Superman persona.

He'd rescued her once, when she'd been hurting and frightened and alone. The rescue had been necessary then —she could justify him carrying her. And no one had been watching.

This rescue was totally unnecessary and pure fantasy. If she let him do this... if she did that, she'd have to accept the fantasy. Admit that she *wanted* the fantasy and also wanted it to be real. And she'd have to do it publicly.

She took a deep breath and slid her arms around his neck. Her pulse was fluttering; her skin was burning with all those eyes on them... but she kept her gaze hard on him and held tight.

A slight smile crossed his face, and then he was hauling the both of them up the steps, taking them two at a time, never once starting to pant. His body was so solid, so strong. She had the sense he could carry her like this forever and never tire, never falter.

Once they were outside, he let her down but kept a grip on her hands. He looked so... *so good*, with his wide smile and the crinkles at his eyes. She ought to be wishing she were invisible just now, with the entire building standing on the sidewalk and staring at them. And she was feeling bashful certainly, her cheeks still quite warm, but it wasn't so bad. Not with Russ staring at her with such a delighted look.

Then Jax came running up to them, giving her a happy

bark of greeting, and the moment went from wonderful to amazing.

"Wow. Fancy meeting you here," she said, trying to be much cooler than she was. She frowned. "Wait, you're not part of the city fire department."

If it was a drill, what was he doing here? And with Jax?

Wait... was all this for *her?*

"Nope." He squeezed her hands. "Called in a favor so I could get your attention."

"I'm pretty sure this is an inappropriate use of municipal resources."

"You can make a complaint with the captain. He's a friend of mine. And right over there."

As he pointed, she caught sight of the engine with a sign stretched across it: *Bea, will you go out with me?*

This *was* all for her. She took in the firefighters, the engine, the entire crowd, and most especially that sign, with her jaw hanging open. This was... Well, she didn't want to repeat the experience anytime soon, but it *was* exhilarating. She could handle this sensation. In small doses.

"You got my text?" she asked.

"You texted me?"

"Yes, just now." But this had clearly been put into motion before that. He was coming for her at the exact same time she had been reaching for him. She didn't believe in coincidence or fate, but it was a bit spooky.

He swallowed hard. "Don't feel like you have to say yes just because I did all this. I only... I wanted to give you proof of how I feel for you. A spectacle for how spectacular you make me feel."

"That..." God, that was possibly the most romantic thing she'd ever heard. And he'd said it to *her.* Her heart swelled until it seemed to be caught in her throat.

"Don't be embarrassed."

"I'm not." She really wasn't. "I'm... thinking."

"Of all the possible reasons why not? Look, you want me to prove to you that how I feel for you is real, that it's not just because I want everyone to like me." His expression was more resolved than she'd ever seen, and it held her with its magnetism. "This is how we build a relationship, a life. In the moments where things are heightened and maddening —not in controlled lab conditions. Yes, we'll have to work out the day-to-day, but we should also savor this. Hot pot and karaoke and sake, and hiking and hippies in the middle of the woods, and a false fire alarm and an entire engine company here to watch me ask you out. Along with everything in between."

She took a deep breath. Wow. First he hit her with the romantic stuff, and then he laid the logic on her. How was she ever supposed to say no to him now?

But first— "You should check your phone."

He frowned and then somehow fished it out of his turnouts. He read the screen and slowly, slowly began to smile.

"I kind of asked you out before you did," she explained, her voice starting to give out on her thanks to all the emotions surging within her. "Not that I don't appreciate all this."

He raised a brow. "Appreciate?"

"Okay, well not quite that far." She was excited and exhilarated, adrenaline coursing through her, but it was also making her dizzy. "I think that once is good for all this." She knew what her answer would be, but committing to it—to him—in front of all these people still wasn't easy for her. "So"—she cleared her throat hard—"would you like to go out sometime?"

His answering grin was daring, cocky. And totally adorable. "How could I say no to hot pot?"

She grinned back at him. "You can't. No one can. I should know."

"What'd she say?" one of the firefighters called to Russ.

Bea looked over and saw that the engine was packing up.

"I told her yes," Russ called back.

"Wait." The firefighter looked confused. "I thought all this was to ask her out. But she asked you?"

Russ turned back to her, his expression alight with devotion. "Yep," he said more quietly. "She came to me."

Bea kissed him then, in full view of everyone, with Jax by their side, because she'd come to Russ once and she could do it again—and she was certain she'd never regret it.

Epilogue

IN THE END, THEIR SECOND date wasn't hot pot.

Bea had suggested that they go to a dog park with Jax instead, which Russ was more than happy to agree to. Jax had been way too depressed without Bea around—he needed some quality time with her too.

Their third date was a hike through the Santa Rosa Plateau, which was enjoyable and shotgun-wielding-hippie-free. Which was a relief, and at the same time a little bit of a disappointment.

Their fourth date was a barbecue at the family ranch, where Bea introduced him to everyone with, "Russ, my boyfriend. He's a firefighter." He'd met Lil, who was delightful, and Fee, who was a little suspicious of him, and all the rest of them.

Between their dates, they'd semi-moved in together, spending the night together at whoever's place was closest. When he was on duty, she worked all hours. And when she had to work late, he went out with the guys or took Jax for a run. For two people with long, odd hours, their schedules meshed pretty well. Russ found that for all of Bea's noise about being inflexible and needing things a certain way, she wasn't really that bad. And he *was* flexible, after all.

Next weekend they were going up to LA to meet his parents. His mother's "I told you so!" was so loud Russ had to hold the phone away from his ear so his eardrums didn't burst.

But this Thursday night for their fifth date, they were finally getting around to hot pot, where it had all begun.

"Do you think the noodles are done?" Bea asked, reaching for one.

Russ caught her chopsticks in his. "Not yet. Here." He laid a piece of pork on her plate. "Eat this."

She snuck a spoonful of soup. "Mmm. We picked the good mushrooms."

"Yep."

"So what happens after this?"

"Once the noodles are done, we eat them." He popped a bite of pork into his mouth. "And then eat some more. And some more."

"And then we pop." She grinned as if she liked that idea.

"We stop before that. Just before we pop, we do some karaoke."

She went still. "Together?"

"A nice romantic duet." He had it all planned—she wasn't likely to drink enough to work up the nerve to do karaoke on her own, but she'd have fun if she belted some tunes out, so he'd help her along.

"Ah. And after that?" She was prodding him for something.

He could guess at what she was really asking. "After that, we go to your house. Or mine." They were comfortable in both places now. "And a few months after that, we start looking for a place together. One that has an easy commute for both of us and, most importantly, will allow both cats and dogs."

She'd been right about the cats—when he'd met them, he'd loved them. Jax loved them too, though the cats weren't so certain about him.

"Hmm." She tapped her chopsticks against her plate. "And after that?"

He saw right through her opaqueness. "Well, sometime next year, I plan on proposing to you. Then we can start planning the wedding. I know a guy who can give us a great deal on a venue."

"Oh? And aren't you forgetting something?" She raised her brow in a dare, but there was an inquisitive spark in her gray eyes.

He checked the noodles—perfect. He ladled out a bowl for her. "You're right. I did forget something."

She scooped some noodles into her mouth and moaned. "Oh, that is good. So what did you forget?"

Time to give this woman he was crazy about another spectacle. But a smaller, more private one. "I forgot that in about a month, I'll tell you I love you."

She paused with a bite halfway to her mouth. "So you think you'll be the first to say it?" But her bravado was weakened by her shock.

"You could always surprise me." He rather wished she would—he'd been holding back the words since their third date, not wanting to scare her off.

"Maybe I will." The words were flippant, but the light shining in her eyes—pleased, winsome—was anything but.

Before he could reply, the music for the karaoke started.

She set down her chopsticks and motioned him out of his seat. "Hurry up," she urged.

"Gonna sing all night?"

"I only want to do the one." But she shook out her hands, nervousness starting to jiggle her limbs.

"Hey. If you don't want to, we won't." He wanted her to enjoy herself, and if this made her more anxious than it did happy, they wouldn't do it.

"I want to and I don't." She made a face. "But I want to more."

"Then we will. Will you hold my hand while we're up there?"

She rolled her eyes, but he could see the teasing behind it. "Come on. Let's do this before I lose my nerve."

They walked up to the stage, hand in hand. She stopped to pick the song and then joined him before all those people. She took his hand again, standing a touch behind him, her gaze sharp on the monitor. He was happy to let her use him as a shield.

He sent a general smile out to the audience, getting ready to entertain them. Most people smiled back—karaoke really was a great way to make people happy.

And then the music started up, and his smile died.

"Oh no." He sent her a betrayed look.

She gave him a wicked grin in return. "Whoops. My finger must have slipped."

"The hell it did. How did they even have this?" Okay, she was clearly not at all embarrassed to do this if she could pick *that* song.

"It's a classic," she said breezily. "Now get ready to sing your heart out, Cheng."

"You first, Schuler."

Just then, "Islands in the Stream" reached its full power. He did sing his heart out, just as much as she did. Because it was silly and he loved that he could inspire her to be silly. And because he meant it too, especially the part about there being nothing between them.

At one point her gaze landed on the audience, and for half a moment her voice faltered. He squeezed her hand and pulled her attention back onto him. *Focus on me. I've got you.*

She ended the song just as strong as she'd started, her gaze locked on his.

When they were finished, the crowd went wild. She ducked her head, her cheeks a deep crimson, but she was smiling. And then she pulled him close, went on tiptoe, and whispered in his ear, "I love you."

He hugged her tight to him since he knew she meant it. Bea wouldn't say that if it weren't true. And held her close for several long moments because his voice wasn't working at the moment, not after she'd knocked him flat like that.

"And your dog too," she went on.

He laughed, a stuttering kind of laugh, because those words filled him so full there wasn't room for anything else.

Pressing a kiss to the top of her head, he said, "Got the drop on me again?"

"Get used to it."

He'd told her to surprise him and she certainly had. He supposed he *had* better get used to it. "I already love it," he said. "And you."

Her breath caught in a sharp gasp as she buried her face in his chest.

"And your cats too," he finished.

"You'd better take me home," she mumbled into his shirt, "before I kiss you here on this stage."

Aww. She was too overcome to even look at him. "Can I do a fireman's lift?"

She shook her head. "No, you got your one embarrassing 'carry Bea' moment. No more. At least not in public."

He could live with that—as long as he got to do it in private. "Well then, let's get you home."

Her home or his home—it didn't matter since they would make it *theirs*.

WANT MORE HOT COWBOY ROMANCE? Pick up *Her Cowboy Rival,* the next in A Cowboy of Her Own! Keep reading for a sneak peek!

About the Author

Genevieve Turner is a *USA Today* bestselling author of western romance. She loves cowboys, the rural life, and happily ever afters. She lives in beautiful Southern California with the perfect number of kids, dogs, and turkeys—and probably too many chickens.

You can find her on the web at www.genturner.com.

Genevieve's Newsletter

NEW RELEASES, SALES, AND A *Free* STARTER LIBRARY WHEN YOU SIGN UP!

CLICK HERE

www.ingramcontent.com/pod-product-compliance
Lightning Source LLC
Chambersburg PA
CBHW030745110726
47900CB00008B/2454